Six vs. Two

"Drink your beer, kid," Clint said. "I've got some thinking to do."

At that moment the batwings slammed open and six men rushed in. Clint recognized Brody and his two friends. He didn't know the other three, but they must have been recruits.

"There!" Brody shouted, pointing at Clint or Starkweather or maybe both of them. The six went for their guns. Customers dove for cover. Clint and Starkweather also drew their guns.

The air was soon filled with the unmistakable sound of lead hitting flesh. Clint made every shot count, putting a slug first in Brody's chest, then in one of the other men. As he shot the third, he readied himself for the onslaught of lead. He turned his gun toward the fourth man, but there were no men standing. All six were on the floor, on their stomachs or on their backs.

He turned and looked at Starkweather. The boy stood tall, didn't seem to have been hit.

"How many shots did you fire?" Clint asked.

"Three," Starkweather said as he reloaded.

"You did pretty good," Clint said to the kid.

"So did you."

"You didn't set that up, did you?" Clint asked. "To prove something?"

Starkweather smiled . . .

DON'T MISS THESE ALL-ACTION WESTERN SERIES FROM THE BERKLEY PUBLISHING GROUP

THE GUNSMITH by J. R. Roberts

Clint Adams was a legend among lawmen, outlaws, and ladies. They called him . . . the Gunsmith.

LONGARM by Tabor Evans

The popular long-running series about Deputy U.S. Marshal Custis Long—his life, his loves, his fight for justice.

SLOCUM by Jake Logan

Today's longest-running action Western. John Slocum rides a deadly trail of hot blood and cold steel.

BUSHWHACKERS by B. J. Lanagan

An action-packed series by the creators of Longarm! The rousing adventures of the most brutal gang of cutthroats ever assembled—Quantrill's Raiders.

DIAMONDBACK by Guy Brewer

Dex Yancey is Diamondback, a Southern gentleman turned con man when his brother cheats him out of the family fortune. Ladies love him. Gamblers hate him. But nobody pulls one over on Dex . . .

WILDGUN by Jack Hanson

The blazing adventures of mountain man Will Barlow—from the creators of Longarm!

TEXAS TRACKER by Tom Calhoun

J.T. Law: the most relentless—and dangerous—manhunter in all Texas. Where sheriffs and posses fail, he's the best man to bring in the most vicious outlaws—for a price.

J. R. ROBERTS

JOVE BOOKS, NEW YORK

THE BERKLEY PUBLISHING GROUP
Published by the Penguin Group
Penguin Group (USA) Inc.
375 Hudson Street, New York, New York 10014, USA
Penguin Group (Canada), 90 Eglinton Avenue East, Suite 700, Toronto, Ontario M4P 2Y3, Canada
(a division of Pearson Penguin Canada Inc.)
Penguin Books Ltd., 80 Strand, London WC2R 0RL, England
Penguin Group Ireland, 25 St. Stephen's Green, Dublin 2, Ireland (a division of Penguin Books Ltd.)
Penguin Group (Australia), 250 Camberwell Road, Camberwell, Victoria 3124, Australia
(a division of Pearson Australia Group Pty. Ltd.)
Penguin Books India Pvt. Ltd., 11 Community Centre, Panchsheel Park, New Delhi—110 017, India
Penguin Group (NZ), 67 Apollo Drive, Rosedale, North Shore 0632, New Zealand
(a division of Pearson New Zealand Ltd.)
Penguin Books (South Africa) (Pty.) Ltd., 24 Sturdee Avenue, Rosebank, Johannesburg 2196,
South Africa

Penguin Books Ltd., Registered Offices: 80 Strand, London WC2R 0RL, England

THE MAN WITH THE IRON BADGE

A Jove Book / published by arrangement with the author

PRINTING HISTORY
Jove edition / July 2009

ISBN: 978-0-515-14652-3

JOVE®
Jove Books are published by The Berkley Publishing Group,
a division of Penguin Group (USA) Inc.,
375 Hudson Street, New York, New York 10014.
JOVE® is a registered trademark of Penguin Group (USA) Inc.
The "J" design is a trademark of Penguin Group (USA) Inc.

PRINTED IN THE UNITED STATES OF AMERICA

10 9 8 7 6 5 4 3 2 1

ONE

The sun did not glint off the star the boy was wearing on his shirt. It wasn't shiny or polished. It wouldn't do any good to polish this star, and nobody would ever call it tin.

So as he rode down the main street of Labyrinth, Texas, nobody really noticed the badge on his chest. Nobody could see it, because it swallowed the sun, didn't reflect it.

He reined in his horse in front of the saloon called Rick's Place. He'd been told he'd find the man he was looking for there.

He tied his horse and went into the saloon. At midday there wasn't much activity. He approached the bar and the bartender looked at him, then looked at his badge.

"What happened to your badge, Deputy?"

"Sheriff," the young man corrected, "and there's nothing wrong with my badge."

"Sorry," the barman said, "no offense. Just thought it looked dirty."

"Can I get a beer?"

"Sure enough, Sheriff," the bartender said. "Comin' up."

The bartender filled a mug and set it down in front of the young lawman.

"I'm looking for a man," he said, after a sip.

"Any man in particular?"

"Clint Adams."

The bartender didn't react.

"The Gunsmith?"

"I know who he is," the barman said.

"Is he around?"

"Can't say."

"Can't, or won't?"

"Look, Sonny—" the barman started.

"Look," the sheriff said, "my age has nothing to do with anything, but this badge does."

"You're out of your jurisdiction," the bartender said, squinting at the badge, "wherever that is."

"Why don't you get me somebody I can talk to," the sheriff said. "Like your boss."

"You're in luck," the bartender said. "The boss is here."

"Good, then get him!"

"Yeah, sure . . ."

Rick Hartman looked up when the knock came on his door. Since he hated any kind of paperwork, he welcomed the opportunity to turn his attention elsewhere.

"Come!"

The door opened and Lew Kelly, his new bartender, stuck his head in.

"Somebody out here lookin' for you, Boss."

"Who?"

Kelly shrugged. "Some kinda weird lawman."

"What makes him weird?" Hartman asked.

"Well, for one thing he looked like he's twelve years old."

That was something Rick had noticed since hiring Kelly. The man didn't like being fifty, and usually took it out on those younger than him. Unless he got that under control he wasn't going to last very long in his job.

"And second?"

"He's wearin' some kinda weird badge."

"What do you mean weird?" Hartman asked.

"Well, it don't got no shine to it," the man said. "Looks kinda . . . dirty. You know? Covered with . . . crud."

"You've got my curiosity up," Hartman said.

"Well, then this'll clinch it," Kelly said. "He's lookin' for your buddy, Clint Adams."

"He asked for him by name?"

"Both of 'em," Kelly said. "Adams and the Gunsmith. What's it like havin' a friend so famous?"

"Well," Hartman said, standing up, "sometimes it gets me out of paperwork. Let's go see what this young lawman wants."

Kelly led the way out of the office.

The young lawman saw the two men approaching and turned to face them, holding his beer in his left hand. He wore his gun on his right hip.

"You looking for Clint Adams?" the second man asked, while the bartender went back behind the bar.

"That's right."

"Rick Hartman. I own this place."

"Must be why it's called 'Rick's.'"

"And what might your name be?"

"Dan Starkweather," the young man said. "Sheriff Dan Starkweather."

"Sheriff of where?"

"A town called Danner, in Kansas."

"Your badge is kind of hard to read," Hartman said.

The lawman smiled.

"That's okay," he replied. "I know what it says."

"What brings you here looking for Clint Adams?" Hartman asked.

"I have a proposition for him."

"You're not looking for a face-off against him, are you?" Hartman asked. "Because if you are, I can advise you not—"

"No, no," Starkweather said, "nothin' like that. I just want to talk to him. Is he around?"

"Well," Hartman said, "he's in town."

"I heard he comes in here a lot."

"Some, I guess."

"Good," Starkweather said, facing the bar again, "then I guess I'll just wait for him."

"You want another beer while you do that?" Hartman asked. "On the house?"

The young man smiled and said, "I never turn down free beer."

TWO

Clint rolled the woman over, buried his face between her big sweet-smelling breasts, and buried his rigid cock between her thighs. Not inside her, though, not yet. Just between her big thighs. It still felt really good, though, rubbing his cock between her thighs while he nursed on her chewable nipples.

That's when the knock came at the door.

"Damn!" he swore.

She held him tightly when he tried to move.

"I've got to get that," he said.

"If you were inside me," she said, "I wouldn't let you go."

He smiled, kissed her, and slid free of her thighs. He pulled on his trousers and went to the door. It was Rick Hartman.

"I've got a lawman at my place waiting to see you," the saloon owner said.

"Who is it?"

"Young fella named Starkweather. You know him?"

"I know that name," Clint said. "But in my memory it doesn't go with a young face. What's his first name?"

"Dan."

"Uh-uh," Clint said. "I don't know him. Guess I better come on over and see what he wants."

"Clint?" the woman called out. "I'm getting cold."

Hartman smiled.

"There's no reason you have to hurry," he said. "He said he's going to wait until you get there. I just figured you needed to know what you were walking into, so I slipped out the back."

"Okay," Clint said. "I'll finish up here and then come over for a drink."

"I'll see you then."

Clint closed the door and turned to face the woman on the bed. She had her hands up over her head, pulling her big breasts taut.

"Either get over here or throw me a blanket."

"Well," he said, "I don't seem to have any blankets, so . . ."

Sheriff Dan Starkweather nursed his third beer. He didn't want to be drunk when Clint Adams showed up. He figured since Rick Hartman had done a disappearing act, he had probably slipped out the back to warn Adams that somebody was waiting for him. Starkweather didn't mind if Adams knew he was waiting.

The saloon began to fill with more men as the afternoon wore on. Starkweather got a spot at one end of the bar and stayed out of everyone's way. Up close his badge was catching some stares, but nobody said a word—not yet, anyway. He knew his youth and the odd sight of his badge sometimes made him the target of some ridicule.

Usually, it was just somebody having fun, but sometimes it escalated into something dangerous. He hoped that wouldn't be the case here.

Just then three men entered the saloon, looked around, and approached the bar. Starkweather had not been wearing his badge for very long, but he knew men on the prod when he saw them. These three were obviously looking for some action, or some trouble.

They elbowed their way to the bar and loudly ordered three beers. Starkweather hoped they wouldn't look over at him, but he had been in Rick's Place long enough for the trouble to be inevitable.

And then one of three did look over at him, and nudged his buddies.

Here we go, Starkweather thought.

THREE

The woman's name was Laurie, and Clint had met her in Rick's saloon. She didn't work there, and she wasn't a whore. She had simply come in to get a drink. Immediately, the men in the place had surrounded her, and Clint took it upon himself to cut her from the herd for himself. He bought a bottle of whiskey for them and invited her to his room, where it was quiet. She accepted. That's where they had been since the night before. The whiskey had run out long before they lost interest in sex and went to sleep.

But sleep didn't last long. He woke that morning with the big-breasted blonde between his legs, rolling his cock between her tits until it was good and hard, and then taking it into her mouth. She sucked him then, until he exploded into her mouth with a roar.

They continued to have sex during the day until Rick Hartman showed up at the door.

When he went back to bed with Laurie, Clint resumed the position he had been in, stretched out on top of her. She'd been lying. She wasn't cold at all, she was burning hot.

This time when he slid his penis between her thighs, he found her vagina wet and waiting. He plunged into her right to the root and she gasped, brought her legs up around him, and held on tightly.

"Oh, God," she gasped as he fucked her. "Oh, yeah, just like that, don't stop, Clint, don't . . ."

And he didn't stop, not until they were both exhausted . . .

She watched him get dressed and asked, "When will you be back?"

"I probably won't be long," he said. "When I come back, we'll get something to eat."

"Good," she said. "I'm starved."

"And then over supper," he said, "We can get to know a little about each other."

She laughed. "We ain't done much talking, have we?"

"No, we haven't."

He strapped on his gun and headed for the door.

"Aren't you going to kiss me good-bye?"

"No," he said. "If I touch your skin, I won't leave this room."

As Clint was going out the door, she yelled, "That might be the nicest thing anybody's ever said to me!"

"What's wrong with yer badge?" one of the three men asked.

Starkweather thought about ignoring them, but he knew that wouldn't work. It never did.

"There's nothing wrong with it," Starkweather said. "It's just the way I like it."

"I ain't never seen a badge like that," a second man said around a huge chaw of tobacco.

"What's it made from?" the third man asked.

"Iron."

"An iron badge?" the first man asked. "That's why it ain't got no shine."

"Is it real?" the man with the chaw asked.

"Yes," Starkweather said.

"No, it ain't," the third man said. "It can't be. If it was real, it'd be a tin star, like all the rest."

"This one is special," Starkweather said.

"How so?" the first man asked.

"Had it made for myself."

"Tol' ya it wasn't real," the third man said.

"Oh, it's real," Starkweather said. "When I got the job, I had a blacksmith make me the badge."

"I say it ain't real!" the third man said.

"Yeah, me, too," the man with the chaw said.

"Hear that?" the first man said. "We don't none of us think it's real. That means if we was to take you, we wouldn't be takin' no lawman."

"Now, why would you want to do that?" Starkweather asked.

"Look atcha," the man with the chaw said. "You ain't old enough ta drink let alone wear a badge. And yer lookin' at us like yer better than us."

"I'm not looking at you at all," Starkweather said. "In fact, you started the conversation, not me."

"I say we take 'im," the third man said.

"Me, too," the man with the chaw said.

"That would be a bad idea," Starkweather said.

"Why?" the first man asked.

"Because if you try to take me, I'll have to kill you."

"All three of us?" the man with the chaw laughed.

"That's right," Starkweather said. "All three of you. It would only be fair."

FOUR

As the three men stepped away from the bar, everyone in the saloon knew there was going to be trouble, so they started moving out of the way. Some of them overturned tables to hide behind.

"Now wait a minute!"

Rick Hartman moved quickly, positioning himself between the three men and the sheriff with the iron badge.

"This is my place and I'm not about to have it busted up," he said.

"You don't get outta the way," the first man said, "a lot more than your place is gonna be busted up."

"Look," Hartman said, "this man is an officer of the law."

"That badge ain't real," the man with the chaw said. "I ain't never seen no iron badge."

"It's real," Hartman said. "If you kill him, you're killing a lawman. They'll never stop hunting you."

The three men looked confused.

"You better step aside, Mr. Hartman," Starkweather said. "Only one thing will stop these men."

"You think you can stop us?" the first man asked.

"It's my job."

"Not in this town it ain't," Hartman said. "You may be a lawman, but you don't have jurisdiction in this town."

"Okay, saloon owner," the first man said. "Time for you to make a move."

"Go ahead, Rick," another voice said. "Move out of the way."

Eyes turned to the batwing doors. Clint Adams had entered quietly and was standing right in front of the doors.

"Your name's Brody, isn't it?" he asked the spokesman of the three.

"That's right."

"You know who I am?"

"Yeah, sure," Brody said, "you're Clint Adams."

"I came over here to talk with this young fellow," Clint said, indicating Starkweather. "And when I get here I find you trying to kill him."

"Well, we—"

"If you kill him," Clint went on, "I wasted my time coming here, and I hate to waste my time."

Brody exchanged glances with his two compadres.

"So go ahead," Clint said. "Make your play, but if you kill him, I'm going to be upset, because I still have to talk to him. And then you'll have to deal with me before you can leave this saloon."

The three men stared at him.

"Time to make a decision," Clint said.

They looked at Starkweather. Rick Hartman had stepped out of the way.

"Like he said, gents," Starkweather said. "Time to make your decision."

There was a long moment of pregnant silence, and then Brody started toward the door. His two compadres followed him.

As they passed Clint, he said in a low voice, "Don't come back here . . . ever."

Brody nodded and left, his two friends right behind him.

Clint approached the bar, waved at the bartender, and said, "Cold beer."

"Comin' up."

Hartman came up next to Clint and said, "Thanks. You cost me two customers."

"How did I do that?"

"You didn't have to tell them not to ever come back here."

"Sorry," Clint said. "I thought I did." He turned to look at the young lawman. "Beer?"

Starkweather looked at the one in his hand. It had gone warm and flat.

"Sure."

Clint turned to Hartman.

"Rick? Join us?"

"No," Hartman said. "I'll leave the two of you to get acquainted. I need to get my business back to normal."

"Suit yourself."

As the bartender gave Starkweather a fresh beer, Clint walked down to join him at the end of the bar.

"I'm Clint Adams," he said. "I understand you want to talk to me."

"Sheriff Dan Starkweather," the young man said. "Danner, Kansas."

"Danner? I don't know it."

"It's about five miles east of Ellsworth," Starkweather said. "It's not much."

"But you're the sheriff?"

"That's right."

"Danner got a telegraph office?"

"It does."

"And if I sent a telegram, I'd find out you're telling the truth?"

"Yes, sir."

"Okay then," Clint said. "Drink up and tell me what's on your mind."

FIVE

"My name's Dan Starkweather," the sheriff said. "That mean anything to you?"

"Well," Clint said, "I've heard the name Starkweather before, but not Dan."

"You've heard of Nathan Starkweather."

"Yes."

"The gunman."

"For want of a better word."

"I have another word to describe him," Starkweather said, "but I don't know if it's better."

"What word is that?"

"Father."

"Ah."

"Yes," Starkweather said, "ah."

"Well, judging from your badge, you haven't taken up the family business."

"No, sir," Starkweather said. "I prefer to walk on the right side of the law."

"Tell me something, son."

"Yes, sir?"

"How old are you?"

"Twenty."

"How did you get to be sheriff?"

"Nobody else wanted the job."

"And what about that badge?"

"What about it?"

"It's a little unusual, don't you think?"

"It's a lot unusual," Starkweather said, "but it won't bend so easy."

"No, I guess it won't."

"So, now I guess I should tell you why I've come looking for you."

"You sound fairly well educated to me, Dan," Clint said.

"I went to a university in the East," Starkweather said. "I came back west when I graduated."

"And what did you study?"

"The law."

"So you're a lawyer?"

"Not yet," he said. "I haven't taken the bar exam yet."

"When do you intend to do that?"

"When I've finished with this."

"And what's this?"

"I was about to tell you," he said.

"Right, right, I interrupted you. But wait, are you hungry?"

"Well, seeing as how I've been standing around here all day drinking beer and waiting for you, yes, I am very hungry."

"Well, at the risk of making a young lady very mad at me," Clint said, "why don't you let me buy you a steak, and we can talk?"

"Sounds good."

They both put the remainder of their beer on the bar and left Rick's Place.

Clint took Starkweather to a restaurant down the street that had opened only a few months ago. It was the first time Labyrinth had ever had something larger than a café. It used to be that each time Clint left town and came back, he enjoyed the fact that he saw no growth in the town. Lately, however, over the past few years, things had begun to change. This restaurant—called Del Rio's—was part of that change.

Clint had been there a few times since it had opened, and they recognized him now when he walked in.

"Welcome back, Mr. Adams. Table for two?"

"Yes, thank you." Clint felt bad that he didn't recall the man's name.

"Henry will be your waiter," the man said.

"Thank you," Clint said again when they were seated.

As they waited for the waiter, Starkweather said, "This looks like a place I used to eat in Philadelphia."

"Yeah," Clint said, "the East and West are starting to blend a little too much for my taste. But I can't deny the food is good."

When a man in a black suit came over to their table, he introduced himself as Henry.

"Two steak dinners, please, Henry," Clint said.

"Right away, Mr. Adams. And two beers?"

"Yes, two beers would be great."

Henry brought the beers quickly, soon followed by the steak dinners. Clint and Starkweather paid strict attention to their meals until they were both about halfway through.

"Okay," Clint said, "I think I'm ready to hear your story now."

Starkweather said, "I think I'm ready to tell it."

SIX

"You don't know what it's like growing up and hearing the stories about your father, the killer," Dan Starkweather said. "My mother sent me to live with members of her family in Philadelphia, and I ended up getting most of my education there. And I was living there when I heard that my mother had died."

"That's tough," Clint said. "I'm sorry."

"You know what's tougher?" the kid asked. "Knowing that your father killed your mother."

"He killed her?"

"Well, I don't mean he pulled the trigger," Starkweather said. "I mean being married to him killed her."

Clint understood that. He'd heard lots of men and women put that kind of blame on a parent.

"My father has run roughshod over the West for as long as I can remember. He's not as well known as you, but he has a more vicious reputation. I read dime novels about him back East. His vicious crimes are well documented."

"Dan, I've had dime novels written about me," Clint

said. "Believe me, you can't believe everything you read in those rags."

"Even if twenty percent of it is true, he needs to be stopped, and nobody seems to be able to do it."

"So you're going to do it?"

"I am," he said. "I knew a town that needed a sheriff, and I went and got the job. And I had this badge made up."

"Why did you have it made out of iron?"

"Because there's something my father does that didn't make it into the dime novels. I know about it, and anybody who knows him knows about it."

"And what's that?"

"Whenever he kills a lawman, he crimps his badge."

"Crimps."

"My father has very strong hands," the boy explained. "He takes a badge in his hand and bends it in two."

"I see what you mean."

"Well," Dan Starkweather said, "he's not going to be able to do that to my badge. So even if he kills me, I'll have the satisfaction of knowing that."

"I see." Clint ate the last piece of his steak and pushed the plate away from him. Henry was at his elbow immediately.

"Anything else, Mr.Adams?"

"Coffee for me, Henry, and a piece of peach pie. Sheriff?"

"I'll have the same," the young lawman said.

"Right away, sir."

Henry removed their plates and went to the kitchen.

"Okay, Dan," Clint said, "this is where you tell me how I fit in."

"My father doesn't ride alone," Starkweather said. "He usually has a gang of about half a dozen men riding with him."

"You want me to come along and take care of them?" Clint asked.

"Well," Starkweather said, "not all of them. I do intend to bring my father in myself, but between the two of us I think we can take care of his gang and get them out of the way."

Clint sat back as Henry arrived with the coffee and pie. When the waiter left, he remained back in his seat, regarding the young man across from him.

"Dan—can I call you Dan?"

"Yes, sir."

"You can call me Clint, not sir."

"Yes, si—Clint."

"What makes you think you've got what it takes to do this?" Clint asked. "And . . . why should I put my life in your hands, because that's what I'd be doing if I threw in with you on this."

"Because," Dan Starkweather said, "the only thing I inherited from my father is his ability with a gun. And, from everything I've heard, I'd put him up against you and give him a good chance."

"Your father's fast, there's no denying that."

"Have you met him? Or gone up against him already? No, if you had, one of you would be dead."

"You're right, I haven't gone against him, and I haven't met him. I just know his reputation."

"And would you be afraid to face him?"

"You know," Clint said, "some good healthy fear can't hurt."

"Then you are."

"It wouldn't matter," Clint said. "Fear's got nothing to do with the way I live. Or with the way your father lives."

"What about the way I live?" Starkweather asked.

Clint leaned forward to cut off a chunk of his pie with his fork and said, "Especially the way you live."

SEVEN

"You didn't see any fear in me with those three yahoos in the saloon, did you?"

"No, I didn't," Clint said. "I should have, but I didn't. You would have stood there and drawn down on the three of them."

"Yes, I would have. And I'd have killed them."

"Without taking a bullet yourself?" Clint asked.

"I think so."

"Eat your pie."

"Will you come with me?"

"I've got to think about it, Dan."

"You are afraid," Starkweather said.

"If that's what you want to believe, then I can't stop you," Clint said.

"We can go outside and I can show you how good I am," the sheriff said.

"How? You going to shoot at some bottles? Some targets?"

"How about we face each other?" Starkweather asked. "If I outdraw you, you come with me."

"And if I outdraw you?"

Starkweather shrugged. "Then I'll go alone."

"I've got a better idea," Clint said. "That is, if you're really sure about your ability."

Starkweather looked suspicious. "What have you got in mind?"

"We face off," Clint said. "Like you said, if you beat me, I go along."

"And if you beat me?"

"You forget the whole thing and go back East, where you belong."

"I don't belong back there!" Starkweather snapped.

"Okay, okay," Clint said, aware that he'd hit a nerve. "So you stay here in the West, but you still forget about bringing your father in."

"I can't do that."

"Why not?"

"I can't let him get away with what he did."

"But if you're so sure you can beat me, where's the risk?"

"There's always a risk," Starkweather said.

"So you don't think you can beat me."

"I think I can," Starkweather said, "but I don't know for sure."

"You can never know anything for sure, kid, until you try," Clint said.

"Come on," Starkweather said. "Do it my way."

"I don't like to draw my gun on a man unless I aim to kill him," Clint said.

Starkweather ignored his pie and chewed on his lips, instead. "Okay."

"Okay you'll do it my way?" Clint asked.

"No," Starkweather said, "but I'll do it for real."

"What?"

"You and me, in the street," Starkweather said. "No contest. For real."

"You'd risk killing me—or being killed—to make your point?" Clint asked.

"Yes."

"But you won't risk . . ." What should he call it? " . . . your quest?"

"No."

"But if I kill you, your father goes scot-free."

Suddenly, Starkweather looked confused.

"Son," Clint said, pushing his chair back, "you better give this a lot of thought before you go any further. I don't think you're thinking straight."

"Wait—"

"Finish your pie and coffee," Clint said. I'll pay the check on my way out. If you want to talk some more, I'll be in the saloon later on. Right now I've got to try to make amends to a lady."

"But Clint—"

Clint walked away without another word and left the restaurant.

"You bastard!" Laurie said when he walked into his room. "You ate something."

"I did," he said, "but I'm here to make it up to you. Come on, I'll take you for something to eat."

"I am dressed," she said, "and I'm not ready to forgive you, so you can stay here while I go get something to eat."

She stormed to the door, then turned and said, "I better not find out you ate with another woman."

As she left, he realized they still knew nothing about each other, and he didn't even know her last name.

EIGHT

Clint was standing at the bar in Rick's Place, nursing a beer and talking to the new bartender, Lew Kelly, when Dan Starkweather came walking in.

"Here's that kid," Kelly said. "I think he's a good one to stay away from."

"Why don't you put a beer on the bar for him, and then you can do that," Clint suggested.

Clint didn't like Kelly. He'd have to tell Rick that before he forgot.

"That for me?" Starkweather asked.

"It is."

Starkweather stepped forward and picked the beer up.

"I wasn't sure if you'd still be talking to me," the kid said.

"Sure, why not?" Clint asked. "No harm was ever done by talking."

"Look," the kid said, "I'm sorry, okay? I don't know what I was thinking, suggesting that we face off. I'm just . . . anxious."

"Do you know where your father is?" Clint asked.

"Exactly? No," Starkweather said, "but I've got a general idea."

"And where would this general idea take you?" Clint asked.

"New Mexico."

"And if I don't go with you, will you go alone?" Clint asked.

"Yes, sir," Starkweather said. "This is something I've got to do."

"Do you think your father will come in with you?"

"No, sir," Starkweather said honestly. "In fact, he might not even believe I'm his son."

"And if he doesn't, he'll try to kill you."

"I guess."

"And there's no way I can talk you out of this?" Clint asked.

For what seemed to be the hundredth time Starkweather said, "No, sir. No way."

Clint sighed.

"Drink your beer, kid," he said. "I've got some thinking to do."

At that moment the batwings slammed open and six men rushed in. Clint recognized Brody and his two friends. He didn't know the other three, but they must have been friends the others had recruited.

"There!" Brody shouted, pointing at either Clint or Starkweather or maybe both.

The six men went for their guns. Customers dove for cover.

Clint and Starkweather drew their guns.

The air was filled with hot lead, smoke, the sounds of

breaking glass, and the unmistakable sound of lead hitting flesh.

Clint made every shot count, putting a slug first in Brody's chest, then in one of the other men. As he shot the third, he readied himself for the onslaught of lead. He turned his gun toward the fourth man, but noticed that there were no other men standing. All six were on the floor, either on their stomach or their back.

He turned and looked at Starkweather. The boy stood tall, didn't seem to have been hit.

"How many shots did you fire?" Clint asked.

"Three," Starkweather said as he reloaded.

Same amount he had fired.

People started getting themselves up off the floor. Lew Kelly crawled out from behind the bar, and Rick Hartman came running from his office, gun in hand.

"Easy, Rick," Clint said. "It's all over."

"What the hell—"

"Brody came back with his friends, and with some help," Clint said. "Guess he figured they had the numbers on their side."

"You gunned all six?" Hartman asked.

"I fired three shots," Clint said, "and so did my friend."

Hartman walked over to the fallen bodies, checked them each.

"All dead," he said, "plugged dead center. Come on, boys, give me a hand getting these bodies out of here." He looked at Clint and Starkweather. "Go wait in my office. I'll handle the law."

Clint turned to retrieve his beer, and found that a stray bullet had shattered the mug.

"Kelly!"

"Comin' up, Mr. Adams."

Clint and Starkweather sat in Rick Hartman's office and drank their beer.

"You did pretty good out there," Clint said to the younger man.

"So did you."

"You didn't set that up, did you?" Clint asked. "To prove something?"

Starkweather smiled. "No, sir, but now I'm wondering why I didn't think of it."

Clint also approved of the way Starkweather had quickly replaced the spent shells in his gun with live rounds before he holstered it.

"Okay," Clint said.

"Okay . . . what?" Starkweather asked.

"I'll go along with you on this . . . quest of yours," he said.

"All ri—"

"But there have to be some ground rules."

"Name them."

"Give me some time," Clint said, "I'll think of some. You got a horse?"

"I do."

"Okay. You want to leave in the morning?"

"I'm ready now."

Clint swirled the beer at the bottom of his mug and said, "Tomorrow will be soon enough, kid."

NINE

Clint stayed in Rick's Place after the front doors were closed and locked.

"Need me for anything else, Boss?" Kelly asked.

"No, Lew," Hartman said. "Go on home."

"Okay," Kelly said. "Night, Mr. Adams."

Clint just waved his hand.

Hartman followed the bartender to the front doors and locked them behind him.

Clint moved around behind the bar.

"You want a beer?" he asked.

"Sure."

Hartman approached the bar and Clint set a mug of beer in front of him.

"I don't like that guy," he said.

"Can't say I'm crazy about him, either," Hartman admitted.

"Why don't you fire him?"

"He hasn't given me any reason to," Hartman said. "He does his job."

"Poor reason not to fire somebody."

"What are you mad at?" Hartman asked. "Or who?"

"Well, for one thing I don't like killing people, so I'm mad about that."

"Then be mad at the dead men, don't be mad at me," Hartman said. "What else?"

"The kid."

"What about him?"

"His father's name is Nate Starkweather."

"Well, I'll be . . . and is he on the level? I mean, with that badge?"

"I only have his word for it, but yeah, I think he's on the level."

"So what's he want with you?"

"He wants to go after his father."

"For what?"

"To bring him in."

"So, tell him to go ahead. Why does he need your blessing?"

"He wants me to go with him."

"What for? Do you know Nate Starkweather?"

"No, but he'll have a gang with him."

"So he handles the father and you handle the gang?" Hartman asked. "Sounds a little uneven to me."

"He handled himself okay tonight," Clint said.

"Oh hell," Hartman said. "You've already made up your mind, haven't you?"

"Yeah."

"You're going with him?"

"Yeah."

"Why?"

"If I let him go alone, it'll be the same thing as shooting him myself."

"I don't follow that logic at all," Hartman said, "but

never mind. I never understand it when you take a hand in somebody else's trouble. When are you leaving?"

"In the morning."

"Does he know where his old man is?"

"He's got it narrowed down to New Mexico."

"Yeah," Hartman said, "and by the time you get to New Mexico, where will he be?"

"I don't know, Rick," Clint said. "I guess we'll just have to find out."

"Well, I know you well enough to know I can't talk you out of this."

"I'll see you when I get back," Clint said.

"As always, watch your back, my friend."

The two men shook hands, and Clint left the saloon.

TEN

Nate Starkweather watched his men empty the bank safe and fill some bank bags with coin and paper money. Another of his men had the bank employees and a few customers backed against a wall and was keeping them covered.

Nate was staring out the front window, waiting for the arrival of the law. He liked nothing better than watching lawmen run toward him, with the sun glinting off their badges. His mentor, the Mexican gunman Jose Batista, had told him to use that reflected light as targets, and he had spent his life doing just that.

"Here they come!" he shouted. "Right on time. Are we ready?"

"Ready, Boss!" his number one man, Santino, called out.

He had one man out front holding the horses, four men with him in the bank. Three of them came out from behind the tellers' cages with money bags.

"Let's go!" Starkweather called out.

He opened the door and ran out, his men behind him.

He heard a shot from inside the bank, but didn't let that concern him. His only concern was the approaching lawmen, running with their guns out.

"Hold it right there!" the sheriff yelled.

"Mount up!" Starkweather shouted to his men.

As his men grabbed their horses and mounted up, Starkweather stepped clear of the excited animals so he could have a clear shot. He drew his gun and fired two shots. With unerring accuracy each of his bullets drilled a hole in one of the tin stars pinned to the chests of the lawmen. Both men staggered and went down.

Starkweather holstered his gun, mounted his horse, and led his men out of town. He was careful to have all of his men ride their horses right over the bodies of the sheriff and his deputy.

The townspeople of Lost Mesa, New Mexico, watched helplessly as the gang rode out of town.

Nate Starkweather waited until they were several miles outside of town before he raised his hand to halt the gang's progress.

"Think we should be stoppin' here, Boss?" one of the men asked.

"Yeah," another man said. "What about a posse?"

"There won't be any posse," Santino said. "Not for a while. They will need to appoint a new sheriff first."

Starkweather took the time to replace his spent shells with live ones, then holstered his gun.

"Evans, gimme your bag," he said.

Paul Evans looked reluctant to part with his bag of money, but Santino went over and grabbed it from him, carried it to Starkweather.

"Walker," Starkweather said. "Your bag."

"Sure, Boss."

Walker dismounted, and carried his bag to his boss.

"Santino, you take Ryan's bag."

Santino did as he was told. Now he had two bags tied to his saddle, and so did Starkweather. A man named Leo Vail had the fifth bag.

"Okay, now we split up," Starkweather said. "The four of you ride west, while Santino and me ride north. Then we all circle around and meet in that canyon. Got it?"

"We got it," Vail said. "Let's go, boys."

Walker and Evans remounted, and the four men turned their horses and rode west.

"Why did you let them keep one bag?" Santino asked. "They might just keep going."

"Did you see which bag I left them?" Starkweather asked. "Vail filled it from the tellers' cages. There ain't enough there for a five-way split."

"Maybe they'll fight over it," Santino said. "End up killing each other."

"Nobody but Vail is worth a damn," Starkweather said.

"How smart can he be if he filled his bag from the tellers' cages?"

"Because he knew I'd let him keep that bag," Starkweather said. "If the others try to take it from him, he'll kill them."

Santino grinned.

"That is what you want," he said, shaking his head. "If Vail kills them, then we have a three-way split of this money."

"And if they all meet us in that canyon, we have enough money for a six-way split," Starkweather said, "although it won't be an even split, will it?"

"Is it ever?" Santino asked.

"Mount up, Mex," Starkweather said. "We left some grub in that cabin in the canyon, didn't we?"

"Food and whiskey, amigo."

"Food and whiskey," Starkweather said, "and bags of money. Can life get any better?"

ELEVEN

The first night in New Mexico they camped by a water hole. Clint made the fire and cooked some beans. Starkweather saw to the horses. He had learned how to handle Eclipse without losing a finger.

When Starkweather joined him by the fire, Clint handed the young lawman a plate of beans and a tin cup filled with coffee.

"You never sent that telegram, did you?" Starkweather asked around a mouthful of beans.

"What telegram is that?"

"The one checking to see if I was really the sheriff of Danner."

"Oh, that telegram," Clint said. "No, I never did get around to that."

"So you believe me?"

"I don't think a man would go to the trouble of having a badge made out of iron and then lie about it," Clint said. "I've decided to take you at your word."

"Thank you," Starkweather said.

"What part of New Mexico do you expect to find your father in?" Clint asked.

"If I know anything about the man, it's that he can't help himself. He has two weaknesses."

"What are they?"

"Banks," Starkweather said, "and killing lawmen."

"Well," Clint said, "I guess if he's done that lately, the word will get around."

"That's what I figured," Starkweather said. "Next town we come to, we might hear word."

They finished eating and had more coffee. Both of them were careful not to stare into the fire. They weren't being tracked, but they still didn't want to ruin their night vision.

"There's something else about that iron badge, isn't there, Dan?" Clint asked. "Something you're not telling me."

"Yes."

"Do you want to tell me now?"

"My father has this habit," Starkweather said. "When he kills a lawman, he likes to shoot him right through his badge."

"And you think the iron badge will protect you against a bullet?"

"He won't be able to crimp it," Starkweather said. "Maybe he won't be able to shoot through it."

"It's a possibility, I guess," Clint said. "Depends on the caliber of the ammo, and the range."

"And I guess I wouldn't mind if people started calling me the man with the iron badge."

"A reputation," Clint said.

"What's wrong with that?" Starkweather asked. "You've got one."

"And it's not something I went looking for," Clint said.

"Well," the younger man admitted, "it's really not high on my list."

"I thought there was only one thing on your list," Clint said.

"You're right," Starkweather said. "Stopping my father, and his gang."

"I'll take first watch tonight," Clint said. They'd been taking turns on watch, just to be safe.

"Okay," Starkweather said. "See you in four hours."

The young lawman rolled himself in his blanket, first removing his gun, but keeping it close. Clint had told him their first night out not to sleep with his gun belt on. There was always the chance of rolling over and shooting yourself. Clint recalled a man who had not only shot himself, but set his pants on fire at the same time. Talk about a rude awakening.

Clint dumped the remnants of coffee from the pot, cleaned it out, and then put an extra handful of coffee in the pot this time. He enjoyed strong coffee, but he didn't think the kid would be able to handle it. Not many men had been able to handle Clint's strongest trail coffee.

The horses nickered, but Clint didn't think anything of it. Probably some kind of critter outside the circle of light given off by the campfire. Eclipse would kick up a fuss if there was anything to worry about.

He poured himself a cup of coffee when it was ready, then decided to clean his gun while he was on watch. While he did, he kept his rifle close, just in case.

Dan Starkweather watched while Clint Adams cleaned his gun. It had taken several days of traveling with Clint before he felt comfortable enough to sleep, effectively turning his back on Adams. By now, though, he pretty much trusted the man, although he was still curious about him. He was learning things from him every day, and it still took him a while to fall asleep on the ground.

Tracking his father was a responsibility, but after this Starkweather didn't think life on the trail was for him.

TWELVE

The first town they came to was called Artisia. They had a newspaper and a telegraph office, and Clint and Starkweather dismounted and split up to find some information. They agreed to meet at the hotel they had passed on their way in.

Starkweather went to the telegraph office, while Clint went to the newspaper office. He entered, and didn't even need to say anything. There were newspapers stacked everywhere. He took one and saw the story on the front page about a bank robbery where a teller and two lawmen were killed. The people of Lost Mesa did not know if the gang had a name, but oddly, both lawmen had been shot right through their badges.

"Can I help you?" a middle-aged man with ink-spotted fingertips asked.

"That's okay," Clint said. "I found out what I came to find out. Do you mind?" He held the newspaper up questioningly.

"Go ahead, take it."

"Thanks."

"It's in the newspaper," the telegraph key operator told Starkweather, "but yeah, we got a telegram from the mayor of Lost Mesa. Wanted to know if our sheriff would form a posse and go after them."

"And did he?"

"Our sheriff?" The man made a face. "We're lucky that gang didn't pick our bank. He wouldn't've gone after them even then."

"Okay," Starkweather said, "much obliged."

"You after that gang yerself, are ya?" the man asked, staring at Starkweather's iron badge.

"I wasn't when I got to town," Starkweather said, "but I think I am now."

"Lemme give ya some advice."

"Okay."

The thin, middle-aged man leaned forward and lowered his voice, as if there were other people in the room, which there were not.

"Don't count on our sheriff for any help."

"I'll remember," Starkweather said, lowering his voice to match. "Much obliged."

"Sure thing."

Starkweather started for the door, then stopped.

"Do you know if Lost Mesa has replaced their sheriff yet?"

"Not that I heard," the man said. "And the operator in Lost Mesa woulda told me."

"Obliged," Starkweather said again, and left.

* * *

Clint and Starkweather met in front of the hotel, went inside, and got rooms. Starkweather had his own money, although he'd never told Clint where it came from. He had offered to cover Clint's expenses, since he had asked Clint to go along, but Clint waved the offer away.

They collected their keys, put their gear in their rooms, and then walked to the nearest saloon. Once they each had a beer, they exchanged notes.

"Looks like we both got the same information," Clint said.

"I didn't hear about the holes in the badges," Starkweather said. "That clinches it for me. So I guess we're going to Lost Mesa."

"I guess we are. I thought I'd talk to the sheriff here, though, before we do that."

"The word I got from the telegraph operator was not to depend on the sheriff for anything."

"Well, there's no harm in talking to him."

"Also, it doesn't seem that Lost Mesa has replaced their sheriff."

"They probably figure that would be like closing the barn door after the horse is already gone."

"Still, they're going to need some kind of law."

"Do they have a mayor?"

"Yes," Starkweather said, "the operator said that the mayor sent a telegram here asking for help."

"Didn't get it?"

"Didn't get it."

"Okay," Clint said. "I'll go and talk to the sheriff."

"Should I come with you?"

"Do you want to spend any time explaining about your badge?" Clint asked.

"No."

"Then why don't you stay here, stay out of trouble, and I'll be right back."

THIRTEEN

Clint entered the sheriff's office, and found a deputy sitting behind the desk with his feet up.

"I'm looking for your boss."

"What's it about, sir?" the younger man asked.

"It's a courtesy call," Clint said. "My name is Clint Adams."

The deputy's feet dropped to the floor and he stared at Clint.

"If I was to guess, I'd say he was at Leo's."

"What's Leo's?"

"A small hotel at the far end of town," the deputy said.

"Is your sheriff a drunk?"

"No," the deputy said, "Leo and the sheriff, they're friends. Mostly the sheriff drinks coffee."

"Okay," Clint said. "What's the man's name?"

"Oh, uh, Sheriff Phipps, Billy Phipps."

I'll go and see if the sheriff is at Leo's. You want me to tell him you had your feet up on his desk?"

"Oh, no sir . . ."

"Don't worry, son," Clint said, "your secret is safe with me."

Clint walked all the way down to the far end of town and found the little place called Leo's. There was half a sign over the door, as if it had once said LEO'S SALOON, but the word SALOON had fallen off.

He entered, found only two men there, one behind a makeshift bar that looked like it was made from several wooden doors, and one customer, who was wearing a badge. They both looked to be in their forties, and they both had the same look on their faces and the same slump to their shoulders. Tired.

"Sheriff Phipps?" Clint asked.

"That's me," the man said. "Help ya?"

"Give the man a minute, Billy," the bartender said. "I don't get that many customers ya know. Beer, friend?"

"Sure."

The man who must have been Leo happily drew Clint a beer and set it on the bar. Clint was surprised to find it cold. There must have been something else about Leo's—or about Leo—that kept customers away.

"That's good beer," he said.

"Thanks."

"What's your name, friend?" Phipps asked.

"Clint Adams."

"The Gunsmith?" Leo asked.

"That's right."

"Jesus, man, that beer is on the house. Whataya think of that, Billy? The Gunsmith in my place."

"Shut up a minute, Leo," Phipps said. "What brings you to my town, Adams?"

"Passing through, Sheriff," Clint said, "but I thought I'd just make a courtesy call and introduce myself."

"That's it? Just a courtesy call?"

"Well, I am curious about something I've been hearing since I came to town a little while ago."

"What's that?"

"Some excitement in a town called Lost Mesa?"

"Oh, yeah," Leo said, "that was somethin'—" He stopped when the sheriff gave him a look.

"Go wait on your other customers, Leo," Phipps said to him.

Leo gave his friend a look and said, "That was just mean."

He moved down to the other end of the bar to sulk.

"Why are you interested in what happened in Lost Mesa?" the sheriff asked.

"I heard they lost a couple of lawmen," Clint said. "Since Lost Mesa's not far from here, I thought I'd volunteer my services if you were putting together a posse."

"And what makes you think I'd be putting a posse together?"

"Well, they got some dead lawmen in Lost Mesa, so you're the closest law."

"That ain't my town."

"I know that," Clint said. "I just thought you'd be volun—"

"With a gang like that on the loose, I ain't about to leave my town unprotected, Mr. Adams. Sorry, but I ain't lookin' for a posse."

"Uh-huh, I see. Well, then I guess I'm wasting my time." He drank half the beer down and slapped the mug down on the makeshift bar. "Thanks for the beer."

"Anytime!" Leo yelled.

"Adams," Phipps said as Clint reached the door.

"Yes?"

"If you're thinkin' of trackin' them bank robbers, don't. Leave it to the law."

Clint spread his arms and said, "That's all I was trying to do, Sheriff."

FOURTEEN

"So?" Starkweather asked Clint when he walked into the saloon.

"Who told you the sheriff would be useless?" Clint asked. He caught the bartender's eye and pointed to Starkweather's beer.

"The telegraph operator."

"Well, he was right," Clint said. "He's going to be no help at all."

"So what's our next step?"

"Tomorrow we'll ride to Lost Mesa, talk to the people there. Then we'll see if we can pick up your father's gang's trail."

"Can you track?"

"I'm no expert," Clint said, "but six men leave a big trail."

"Because I don't know anything about tracking," Starkweather said.

"I'll teach you whatever I know," Clint said, "but I'm warning you, that won't take long."

"Do you know anyone who can track?"

"I know a lot of great trackers," Clint said. "Unfortunately, none of them are in New Mexico right now. At least, not that I know of."

There was a disturbance in the saloon at that moment. A couple of men in a poker game started a fight, and ended up turning the table over and rolling on the floor, but it didn't look like there was any gunplay involved.

"You're wearing the badge, kid," Clint said. "You want to do anything about that?"

"This town's got a sheriff," Starkweather said. "I'm going to get something to eat and then go to my room."

"You got any hell-raiser in you, Dan?" Clint asked

"Not that kind," Starkweather said, indicating the men rolling around on the floor.

"You strike me as a very serious young man."

"Once I've brought my father in," Starkweather said, "maybe I'll try to relax a little, but not before."

"Okay," Clint said. "Let's finish these up and, like you said, get something to eat."

"We going to get an early start tomorrow?" Starkweather asked.

"Bright and early, kid," Clint said. "Bright and early."

"What the hell?" Leo said after Clint left his place. "What is Clint Adams doin' around here?"

"Sounds like he's gonna butt his nose in where it don't belong," Sheriff Phipps said.

"You gonna warn Nate Starkweather?"

"That's how I keep him outta my town, ain't it?" Phipps demanded.

Leo Kearns smiled.

"Don't pull that with me, Billy," Leo said. "I know about the money he gives you, remember?"

"That's because I spend most of it in here, you old bandit," Phipps said.

Neither of them wanted to admit the truth, that Billy Phipps was scared to death of Nate Starkweather, and that was why he supplied information.

"I guess you'll have to send a telegram," Leo said.

"Yeah, but I'll wait until Adams leaves town," Phipps said.

"How do you think Starkweather will take the news that the Gunsmith is on his trail?"

Phipps blew some air out of his mouth and said, "Let's just say I'll be glad I'm not standing in front of him when I tell him."

FIFTEEN

Lost Mesa was about twenty miles north of Artisia. Clint would have liked to set a brisk pace with Eclipse, but there was no way Starkweather could have kept up. Still, they made good time and covered the twenty miles in less than half a day.

As they rode into town, the townspeople—obviously still smarting from having their bank robbed and their lawmen killed—stayed off the street, and from behind closed curtains stole peeks at the two strangers.

Clint and Starkweather reined in their horses in front of the sheriff's office. When they tried the door, they found it unlocked. As they entered, it became clear that no one had been in there since the sheriff had been killed. In the weeks since the brutal murders of the sheriff and his deputy—and one bank teller, who had apparently been shot for no reason—spiders had been the only inhabitants, and had left behind their webs.

Clint waved some of the webs away with his hands, which he then wiped on his trousers.

"Well it's obvious they haven't filled the job," he said.

"So what do we do?" Starkweather asked.

"As the only lawman in town, you're entitled to use this office."

"Really? Won't somebody object?"

"Let them," Clint said. "We're going to go and see the mayor, anyway. But first we'll take care of the horses. You stay here and I'll put them up at the livery."

"What about rooms?"

"Check out the cells here. If we can clean them, we'll sleep in there."

"Somebody's got to object to that."

"We'll check in with the mayor when I get back."

"But—"

"Hey," Clint said, "you're the man with the badge. If anyone asks, show it to them."

He left before Starkweather could offer any more argument.

By the time Clint returned, Starkweather had found a broom and swept out the office and the two cells in the back.

"I also found some blankets folded up. Haven't been used in a while, but we can use them."

"Good. Anybody come in?"

"No. You talk to anyone?"

"Just the liveryman," Clint said. "He's afraid of strangers. I had to convince him I wasn't here to kill anybody."

Starkweather put the broom aside. "See any place to eat?"

"A few places, actually. But one in particular appealed to me."

"Why is that?"

"It looks like the biggest place in town," Clint said. "Where most of the people would eat."

"We going there?"

"No," Clint said. "At least, not now. We'll catch a bite at one of the other places, but then we'll go to this place for supper."

"Okay."

"Meanwhile, let's go talk with the mayor first, before we get that bite."

"Okay," Starkweather said again.

Before they could speak to the mayor, they had to find out who the mayor was. Clint decided to get one beer in the first saloon they came to and ask the bartender.

When they entered the saloon, heads turned to take them in. There were about a dozen men in the place, but as Clint and Starkweather approached the bar, about eight or nine of them headed for the door.

The bartender eyed them warily.

"What's wrong with everyone?" Clint asked.

"Uh, we're a little afraid of strangers in this town since the, uh, robbery."

"Two beers," Clint said.

"Comin' up."

As the bartender set the beers on the bar, his eyes fell on Starkweather's badge.

"What's that?"

"That's my badge."

"Is it real?"

"It's real," Clint said. "What's your name?"

"Wilson."

"That your last name, Wilson?"

The man shook his head.

"First name."

"Okay, Wilson. It looks to us like your sheriff hasn't been replaced yet."

"Nobody wants the job," Wilson said. "Not after what happened to the sheriff and his deputy."

"And what did happen, exactly?"

"They were shot down in the street," Wilson said, "and then when the gang rode out, they rode right over their bodies."

"Jesus," Starkweather said.

"When we got to them, they was all busted up," Wilson went on, "and they were shot right through their badges. It was the damndest thing I ever saw."

"Okay," Clint said, "I guess I can understand why nobody wants the job."

"Yeah."

"Wilson, can you tell me the mayor's name? And where to find him?"

"Sure," Wilson said. "You want the job?"

"No," Clint said, "but we do want to talk to the mayor."

"Well, his name is Ralston, Jack Ralston. Everybody just calls him Mayor Jack."

"Cute. Where can I find Mayor Jack?"

"He's got an office on Main Street," Wilson said. "Attorney-at-law. You can't miss it. It's painted on the big front window."

"Okay, Wilson," Clint said. "Thanks."

"Sure."

"Sorry we emptied your place out," Clint said.

"Hell, they'll come back."

Clint nodded, then he and Starkweather left.

SIXTEEN

As the bartender had promised, the office of Jack Ralston, attorney-at-law, was not hard to find. Clint opened the door and stepped in, with Starkweather right behind him. Clint expected to find a secretary, but instead found a man seated at a desk, with law books on the wall behind him. His jacket hung on the back of his chair, and the sleeves of his white shirt were folded up over his healthy-looking forearms.

"Gents, can I help you?" he asked. "Which of you needs representation?"

"Neither one," Clint said. "This is Sheriff Dan Starkweather, and I'm Clint Adams. We'd like to talk to you as mayor of this town."

"You are the Gunsmith, aren't you?"

"That's right."

"What can I do for you in my capacity as mayor, sir?" Mayor Jack asked.

"We heard and read about the incident that happened here a little more than a week ago."

"Incident?" Mayor Jack asked. "If you can call bank robbery and murder an incident."

"Has anyone from this town gone after the gang?" Clint asked.

"No," Mayor Jack said. "We lost our lawmen, and no one was willing to take over—especially if it meant taking a posse out after them. That gang was vicious. They shot a teller in cold blood."

"Was the gang in town for any period of time before they took the bank?" Clint asked.

"I don't know," Mayor Jack said. "That's the kind of thing the sheriff would know, isn't it?"

"It is," Starkweather said.

Mayor Jack looked at Starkweather, then looked again.

"Is that a badge?"

"It is."

"What's it made from?"

"Iron."

"An iron badge?" Mayor Jack looked at Clint. "Is that for real?"

"It's for real," Clint said, "but never mind that. Was the deputy who was killed the only deputy in town?"

"No," Mayor Jack said, "we had another one. He resigned rather than take the sheriff's job." Suddenly, Mayor Jack gave Starkweather a different look. "You happy with your job? You want to be sheriff here?"

"I'm happy."

"What town are you sheriff of?"

"Danner, Kansas."

"Kansas? Why not take this job instead?"

"Mayor Ralston," Clint said.

"Call me Mayor Jack. Everybody does."

"Mayor Jack, we're not here looking for a job. We've already got a job to do."

"What job?"

"We're going to track the gang who killed your sheriff and bring them back."

"And our money?"

"If they still have it."

Mayor Jack looked at them suspiciously. "What do you want in return?"

"Nothing," Clint said. "We're going to spend the night sleeping in your jail and get going in the morning. Does anybody in town have any idea what direction the gang went in?"

"Talk to Eddie Forbes."

"Who's Forbes?"

"Head teller at the bank. He got mad after the gang shot one of the tellers for no reason. After they left the bank, Eddie grabbed a gun from the manager's office and ran out after them."

"That was foolish," Clint said.

"He didn't do any harm," Mayor Jack said, "or good, but he ran after them as far as the end of town. Maybe he knows something."

"Okay," Clint said, "We'll talk to Forbes. Is the bank still open?"

"Yeah," Mayor Jack said, "we managed to bring in some money from another town to keep it going."

"Not Artisia."

"No," Mayor Jack said, "a town west of us called Val Verde."

"Okay, so we'll find Forbes at the bank."

"I guess so."

"Okay, Mayor," Clint said. "If we think of any more questions, can we find you here?"

"Until late—maybe nine p.m. After that I'll be home. I live in a two-story frame house on the north end of town."

"Okay," Clint said. "Thanks."

As they started to leave, Mayor Jack said, "Mr. Adams."

"Yes?"

"I'm sure there are men in this town who would follow you, sir, once they know who you are."

"We're not looking for a posse, Mayor," Clint said. "We'll do just fine by ourselves."

"Are you after a reward?"

"No."

"What's your interest, then?" Mayor Jack asked. "I'm curious."

Clint looked at Starkweather, who shrugged.

"Mayor," the younger man said, "we believe the gang was led by a man named Nathan Starkweather."

"Nathan . . . I know that name, don't I?"

"He has a reputation," Dan Starkweather said. "He's also my father."

"He's a killer."

"Yes," Starkweather said, "he is, and he killed three people in your town. I'll bring him back."

"Here?" Mayor Jack said. "You're going to bring him back here?"

"It's his most recent crime," Starkweather said. "I'll bring him back for trial."

"Here?" Mayor Jack said again. "Wait, he's your father and you're going to bring him back?"

"He's a criminal, and I'm a lawman," Starkweather said. "That's my job."

"Did he commit a crime in your town?"

"He did."

"Then take him back there."

"I will," Starkweather said. "After you're done with him here."

The mayor sat back heavily in his chair. "I don't want him back here."

"Excuse me?" Clint asked.

"We just want the money back."

"He killed your sheriff, a deputy, and a teller," Clint said. "You don't want to try him for that?"

"No," Mayor Jack said. "Besides, we have no lawman, and the jail is closed."

"We reopened it," Clint said.

"I swept it out," Starkweather said.

"Name somebody to the job," Clint said. "Hell, take the job yourself."

"Me?" Mayor Jack looked appalled. "I'm a politician, not a lawman."

"Look, Mayor—" Starkweather started.

"No, this is final," the mayor said. "We won't prosecute Nathan Starkweather or any of his men."

"But you will take your money back," Starkweather said.

"Yes, of course."

Starkweather looked at Clint, unsure about what to do next. Clint shrugged and left the office. Starkweather followed.

SEVENTEEN

Clint and Starkweather went from the mayor's office to the bank. When they entered the bank, there were several sharp intakes of breath. The employees were frightened. No one could blame them.

"Tell them who you are," Clint said, "before somebody pulls a gun out of a draw."

"Ladies and gents, my name is Sheriff Dan Starkweather. We're here to speak with a man named Eddie Forbes. Is he here?"

"I'm Forbes," a man said, from behind a teller's cage.

"Eddie, can we talk to you outside?" Starkweather asked.

Forbes did not move from behind the cage. "Who's he?"

"His name is Clint Adams," Starkweather said. "He's help—"

"The Gunsmith?" a man said, from behind his desk. "You're the Gunsmith?"

"That's right."

"Are you going after the gang that killed Herbert Fowler?" the man asked.

"Herbert Fowler was the teller who was killed?" Clint asked.

"Yes."

"We're going to track the gang, yes," Clint said. "And we intend to bring them and the money back here."

"Why do you n-need to talk to me?" Forbes asked.

"Let's talk outside, Eddie," Clint said, waving. "Come on."

Slowly, the meek-looking man came out from behind the cage. He approached Clint and Starkweather timidly. Clint put his arm around his shoulders and helped him out the door.

"Eddie, we heard that you did a pretty brave thing during the robbery."

"I—I didn't do anything—"

"We heard you ran after the robbers with a gun," Starkweather said.

"I was . . . angry that they had killed Herbert. And then I saw the sheriff and his deputy on the ground—shot, trampled."

"You lost your head."

"Yes, sir."

"You ran after the gang with a gun."

"I did. But I didn't fire it. I-I'm no good with a gun."

"That's okay, Eddie," Clint said. "We just want to ask you one thing."

"W-what?"

"Do you have any idea which direction the gang went when they rode out of town?"

"H-how would I know that?" the man asked, his eyes worried and watering.

"Well, they may have said something while they were in the bank," Clint said, "or you may have seen where they went."

"I—I'd like to help, really I would."

"We're going to be in the jail overnight," Clint said. "We'll be leaving in the morning. If you think of anything you might have heard, or saw, come and see us, Eddie." He put his hand on the man's shoulder. "All we're asking is that you think it over."

"A-all right," Eddie Forbes said, "I will."

"Thanks, Eddie."

After the teller went inside, Starkweather asked, "You really think he knows something?"

"I don't know," Clint said. "I didn't when we walked in there. But he's too nervous. If he knows something, maybe he'll come across."

Clint and Starkweather had decided they would eat their supper in the jail. They stopped in the restaurant to pick it up, and as Clint had figured they would, they attracted attention.

Now they were sitting at the sheriff's desk, eating their steak dinners.

"This isn't bad," Starkweather said.

"Thinking about taking the mayor up on his offer?" Clint asked.

"No," Starkweather said.

"You like Danner that much?" Clint asked. "Nice place to live?"

"I don't live there."

"Where do you live?"

"Nowhere, at the moment," Starkweather said.

"You never told me your father committed a crime in Danner."

"He killed a man," Starkweather said. "I heard about it."

"A man?"

"The sheriff," Starkweather said. "When I heard about it, I rode to Danner. Much like this town, no one wanted the sheriff's job. They're all afraid of my father."

"But you're not."

"I talked to the mayor, and he gave me the job. I supplied my own badge and rode out. I was in Danner for less than three hours."

"How long have you been trying to find your father?" Clint asked.

"Six months."

"You're the sheriff of Danner, Kansas, and you haven't been there in six months?"

Starkweather nodded.

"How do you even know you still have the job?" Clint asked.

"The mayor and me have a lot in common."

"Like what?"

"The sheriff my father killed?"

"Yeah."

"He was the mayor's brother."

"Then why isn't the mayor's ass in the saddle?"

Starkweather laughed. "They don't make saddles wide enough, or horses big enough."

Clint laughed.

"Besides," Starkweather added, "he's a lot like this mayor—he's a politician, not a lawman."

"So what do you plan to do after you bring your father to justice?" Clint asked. "That is what you're planning to do, right?"

Starkweather played with his steak.

"I mean, you do intend to see that he stands trial, right? You're not planning anything silly, like killing him?"

"That'll be his call," Starkweather said.

"And knowing what you know about him, what do you think his call will be?"

"I don't think he'll come along easily."

"You don't think?" Clint asked. "Or are you counting on that?"

"Right now I'm just trying to find him," Starkweather said. "I don't know what will happen when I do."

Clint poured some more coffee for both of them from the office coffeepot they'd found on the stove. It was awful. He didn't know what had been in the pot last, and he didn't want to know.

"When your father does make the call, Dan," Clint said, "I wonder if you'll be able to do what you have to do."

"I guess we'll all find out at the same time," Starkweather said. "God, what was in this pot . . ."

EIGHTEEN

Clint was sitting behind the sheriff's desk with his feet up, and Starkweather was about to go to sleep in one of the cells, when the door opened.

Eddie Forbes stuck his head in.

"Hey, Eddie," Clint said. "Come on in! Have a seat."

"Um, I was wondering if I could have a word with you?" Forbes asked.

"Both of us?" Clint asked.

"Um, yes."

"Like I said," Clint repeated, "come on in."

Forbes came the rest of the way in and closed the door behind him. He was still dressed for work in a tweed suit, white shirt, and tie.

Slowly, he approached the desk. Starkweather pulled a chair over for him. The sound of the chair dragging on the floor startled him.

"Take it easy, Eddie," Clint said. "We're all friends here."

Forbes sat down gingerly, looking as if he might bolt from the room any minute.

"What's on your mind, Eddie?"

"I didn't know anyone would g-get hurt," he said haltingly.

"Did you do something to help the gang rob the bank?" Clint asked.

"I was in the saloon," he said, "and they—they made me sit with them. They made me drink whiskey and—and talk about the bank."

"So you told them how much money was in the bank, how many people worked there, like that?" Clint asked.

"Y-yes," he said. "I—I didn't know why they were asking me those questions."

"Sure you knew, Eddie," Starkweather said. "You had to know."

"How much did they pay you, Eddie?"

"A—a hundred dollars."

"A hundred dollars?" Starkweather asked. "That's what three lives were worth to you?"

"I tell you, I didn't know!" Forbes said. Then he sobbed and buried his face in his hands.

"Eddie," Clint said, "look at me. Come on, Eddie! Look!"

Forbes took his face from his hands and looked up at Clint.

"You need to tell us what you know," Clint said. "Anything that would help us catch the gang."

"I—I don't know anything."

"Sure you do," Clint said. "Or you wouldn't be here. Come on, you heard something."

"Well . . . they talked about a canyon that nobody could ever find. And a cabin."

"Like the Hole-in-the-Wall?"

"Huh?"

"Never mind," Clint said. "Is that where they were going to go after the job?"

"I think so."

"And how far is it?"

"I—I can't be sure, but I think they said it would take several days to get there."

"And then how long were they going to stay?"

"That I—I don't know anything about," Forbes said. "Really."

"Wherever it is," Starkweather said, "they're probably gone now."

"That may be," Clint agreed, "but they may have left something useful behind." He looked at Forbes. "Anything else, Eddie?"

"I—I don't know—"

"Come on, Eddie!" Starkweather said. "Just a little more."

"Well . . . it seemed to me that the gang was separated into two parts."

"Yes?"

"Mr. Starkweather, he was very friendly with a man named Santino. And then the other four men stuck together."

"Santino must be his number one," Clint said. "Like a foreman."

"Any other names, Eddie?"

"One of them was called Vail, but . . . that's all I know. Are you going to put me in jail?"

"I should put you in jail for what you did," Starkweather said, "but I don't have time!"

"Go home, Eddie," Clint said. "Just . . . go home. Don't talk to anyone else about this."

"You—you're not going to tell?"

"No," Clint said, "we're not going to tell."

"Come on, Eddie," Starkweather said, grabbing his arm. "Let me help you out the door."

At the door Forbes looked at Starkweather and said, "I really didn't mean any harm."

"Yeah," Starkweather said, "tell that to your friend Herbert."

He pushed him out the door.

Later, Clint was still sitting at the sheriff's desk when he heard the cot in one of the cells squeak and Starkweather came out.

"Can't sleep?" Clint asked.

"No."

"Me neither."

"Are we doing the right thing, letting Eddie go off scot-free?"

"I don't think he's scot-free, Dan," Clint said. "I think this is going to eat at him for a long time."

"But . . . he practically let them in, helped them kill—"

"Let's not forget who pulled the trigger here, okay?" Clint said.

"Okay," Starkweather said. "So how do we find this Hole-in-the-Wall hideout?"

"The trail is old, but we'll have to try to pick it up," Clint said. "Even if we end up following a trail of cold campfires."

"And how do we do that?"

"Well," Clint said, "we start by getting some sleep. Come on, let's give it another try."

They both went into the cell block, and each into a separate cell.

NINETEEN

"This is hopeless," Starkweather said. "We're almost two weeks behind them."

Clint looked up at Starkweather, who was still mounted.

"Have you been closer to them than two weeks before?" he asked.

"Well, no . . ."

"Then you're better off than you ever were," Clint said.

It was mid-afternoon the next day. They had left town very early. Clint tried to figure out the gang's initial direction. They would have ridden hard, just to put some space between them and town.

"Then they probably would have stopped and split up," Clint said to Starkweather.

"Why?"

"To make themselves harder to track," Clint said. "Eddie said that your father and Santino were tight. I bet your father—"

"Could you stop calling him that?"

"Oh, sorry," Clint said. "I'll be . . . Nate and Santino went one way, and the rest of the gang went in another direction."

"And later they'd meet at their hideout?"

"Right."

"What about the money?"

"I'll bet Nate took most of it."

"So what was to stop him from forgetting all about the meeting and keeping the money to split between him and Santino?"

"He might have done that," Clint said, "but then he'd have to find himself another gang, and the men he cheated would be looking for him. No, as long as he wants to have a gang he'll meet up with them. It won't be an even split, but they'll get more money staying with Nate than going off on their own. They know that."

"They might not even be in New Mexico anymore," Starkweather said.

"That's true, too."

Clint mounted up.

"What do we do?"

"Pick a direction," Clint said, "and keep riding."

"Until when?"

"Until we find out it's the wrong direction."

"How do we just . . . pick one?"

"Okay," Clint said, "they wouldn't go south. That leads back to town. And I don't think they'd go east."

"Why not?"

"That's the way to the closest town, and leads back to Texas," Clint explained. "So, two of them—Nate and Santino—went one way, and the other four another."

"North and west."

"Right."

"And then they'd have to circle around to join up again."

"In their canyon."

They sat their horses and looked north, and then west.

"North," Starkweather said, just as Clint said, "West."

"How do we decide?" Starkweather asked.

"Well, we don't want to sit here all day jawing about it, so . . ."

He reached into his pocket and pulled out a coin. He flipped it, caught it, and smacked it down on his wrist.

"Call it," he said.

"Heads."

Clint looked at the coin.

"Heads it is," Clint said. "We go north."

They found several campfires while riding north, which influenced them to keep going.

"When do we change our minds?" Starkweather asked, two days later.

"Forbes said it was several days' ride," Clint said. "We'll give it another day."

They had stopped in one small town to refresh their supplies—coffee and beans only, because they were traveling light.

They camped their second night out, built a fire, and had something to eat.

"What if they went to Arizona?" Starkweather asked.

"Then we'll go to Arizona."

"We're not exactly tracking them, are we?"

"No," Clint said, "we're too far behind them to track them—unless there was something distinctive in their tracks. If that's the case, and we find their hideout, we might learn about it there."

"What's the original Hole-in-the-Wall like?"

"Lots of different gangs," Clint said, "all with their own supplies."

"What if this one's the same way?"

"Then they'll see us coming," Clint said. "If that happens, I'll be awful glad that you're wearing a badge that doesn't catch the sun."

TWENTY

It was their third day out from Lost Mesa. Late, almost dusk.

"Wait," Clint said. "Stop."

"What is it?"

"Something . . . Stay here."

Clint rode ahead at a slow pace, raking the ground with his eyes.

"What do you see?" Starkweather called.

Clint turned Eclipse so he could look at Starkweather.

"A trail," Clint said, "or a path worn into the ground. You see it?"

Starkweather stared at the ground, then looked ahead. He was about to say no when it came into focus for him. "I see it."

Clint rode back to Starkweather's side, and turned Eclipse so they were facing the right way. There it was—faint, but there.

"Up there," he said, pointing at the foothills ahead of them.

"Not the mountains?"

Clint shook his head.

"Outlaws are lazy," he said. "If there's a canyon in there, it's in among the foothills."

"And it might be filled with outlaws."

"Probably not."

"Why?"

"They would have spotted us by now," Clint said. "Probably would have taken a shot at us, too."

"Maybe they're waiting for us to get closer," Starkweather said.

"Well," Clint said, "we better not keep them waiting."

They found it. There was a fissure in among the hills that was wide enough for them to walk their horses through. Once they got inside the canyon, they found a cabin—just one.

"This is no Hole-in-the-Wall," Clint said. "One cabin, no corrals."

"And nobody around," Starkweather said.

"Let's take a closer look," Clint said.

They mounted up and rode closer.

There were plenty of tracks outside the cabin. Inside there was some worn-out furniture, including a wobbly table that the gang probably ate on. The stove was serviceable, if you had the makings of a fire.

They both walked around the one-room cabin, trying to find something helpful. Starkweather bent over and picked something up.

"What'd you get?" Clint asked.

"These paper bands from the bank," Starkweather said. "So the money was here."

"They made their split here," Clint said. "Took the bags with them, and most of the bands."

"They sure didn't leave anything else behind."

"This doesn't look like a regular hideout," Clint said. "I think they found this place and decided to use it after the robbery. Make their split, maybe spend a few days lying low."

"When they left, they wouldn't leave all at once, right?"

"Right," Clint said. "Nate would give them all instructions about where to meet up with him."

"How come there are no tracks on the floor?" Starkweather asked.

"Over there, in the corner."

Starkweather looked, saw a broom leaning against the wall.

"They swept up after themselves?"

"Took care of any footprints. Come outside with me. Bring the broom."

Clint stepped out. Starkweather grabbed the broom and followed.

Look." Clint took the broom and ran his palms over the bristles. His hand came away covered with dust and some dirt.

"They swept outside, too?" Starkweather asked.

"Wanted to cover not only their tracks, but their horses', too." He handed the broom back. "But I'm betting they missed some."

"Where?"

"That's what we're going to find out, and before it gets dark."

"Where do we look?"

"I'm going to look. You go and find some wood. We're going to spend the night, and we'll need a fire."

"Okay."

Starkweather set the broom aside, leaning it against the wall. He mounted up and rode off while Clint started walking around the outside of the cabin.

TWENTY-ONE

Starkweather returned with plenty of wood. They chose to build the fire inside the oven, thinking it might last longer that way, require less wood to keep it going all night. However, if they did need more, Clint figured they could break up the furniture and use the pieces.

Clint cooked, and soon the cabin was filled with the smell of bacon and beans.

"You find anything we can use outside?" Starkweather asked.

"Maybe."

"Maybe?"

"Depends on how many people have used this cabin," he said. "I was behind the cabin when I decided to take a look a little farther away."

"What'd you find?"

"I found a hole somebody was using as a privy. I found some tracks from somebody who needs a new pair of boots. His left heel is worn down on one side. I'd be surprised if he wasn't walking with a limp."

"Because of it?" Starkweather asked. "Or was it worn down because he limps?"

"Good point," Clint said, "Either way it's something we can use, if he's one of Nate's gang."

Starkweather made a face.

"Is this all you ever eat on the trail?" he groused. "Beans and bacon?"

"No," Clint said, "sometimes I eat plain beans, sometimes plain bacon. If I took a packhorse with me everyplace I went, I'd have more of a variety of food to eat, but I like to travel light, kid."

"Just convinces me even more that I don't want to spend my life on the trail."

"Got some place you want to settle down yet?" Clint asked.

"No," Starkweather said, "I'm just talking."

"Think you'll return to the East?"

"I don't think so."

"Well, you could just go back to Danner and keep the job."

"That's one way to go," Starkweather said, "but I don't know how I'll feel about being a lawman after all this."

"You've got time to make up your mind."

"Because I'm young?"

"No, because it'll take us a while to catch up with your d—I mean, with Nate and his gang."

Clint cleaned off the plates and utensils when they were done, then made another pot of coffee.

"How about some two-handed poker?" he asked, when they were once again seated across from each other.

Starkweather looked sheepish, then said, "I, uh, never really learned how to play poker."

"Is that a fact?" Clint took a worn deck of cards from his saddlebags. "Well, you can't very well survive in the West if you don't know how to play poker. We'll start with five-card stud."

Clint dealt the cards.

"These are certainly worn out," Starkweather said, picking them up.

"I play a lot of solitaire when I'm alone on the trail," Clint said. "I'm sure you do the same."

Starkweather looked sheepish again.

"Damn, boy, but your education surely is lacking."

By morning they had each slept four hours, and Starkweather had learned how to play both solitaire and poker. In fact, Starkweather was sitting up playing solitaire when the sun came out. That was his signal to put the cards down and make a pot of coffee. When the coffee was ready, he went over and nudged Clint.

"Time to get up."

"I'm up."

Clint got to his feet, rolled up his blanket, then came to the table for coffee.

"Black jack on red queen," he said.

"I got it."

Starkweather finished the game while they drank coffee, then Clint said he'd go outside and see to the horses.

By the time he walked the horses around to the front of the cabin, Starkweather was there with their saddlebags and rifles.

Once they were mounted, they sat there for a moment.

"Where to now?" Starkweather asked. "We didn't find anything that would tell us where they're headed."

"I don't think they'd keep going north," Clint said. "Rough terrain, and outlaws—like I said—are lazy."

"So?"

"So we go to Arizona, kid," Clint said. "Ever been to Arizona?"

"No."

"Then don't look so glum," Clint said.

TWENTY-TWO

"I've got to tell you," Starkweather said as they rode into the town of Fenton City, Arizona. "I never expected you to stick with me this long."

"Five weeks since we left Labyrinth," Clint said. "You think that's a long time?"

"Isn't it?"

"Maybe," Clint said, "when you're twenty years old. To me, though, it's not long at all."

"Still," Starkweather said. "Long time for you to be minding somebody else's business."

"Maybe, maybe not."

"We've been riding through Arizona for two weeks," Starkweather said. "What if they're not even in the state anymore."

"We haven't heard anything about their kind of job being pulled," Clint said. "No robberies, no banks, or stagecoaches. They're still in Arizona, Dan. They don't have any reason to leave. They're not wanted here."

"So what are they doing?"

"My bet is they're scoping out a job, waiting for the

right time to pull it," Clint said. "When they do, we'll hear about it."

"So what do we do until then?"

"What we've been doing," Clint said.

"Visiting your friends?" Starkweather said. "You sure know a lot of people. So far I've met a newspaper publisher, a store owner, a rancher—a pretty rancher—and a saloon owner. Who is it this time?"

"Somebody who actually might be able to help us," Clint said. "A lawman."

"The town sheriff?"

Clint nodded.

"Tom Dockery," he said. "Been the law here for about three years. Before that he was a deputy federal marshal. A lot of inmates in Yuma have him to thank."

"Why settle this close to the prison, then?" Starkweather asked. "So he can track escapees?"

"He does that, sure, but I don't think that was his goal. He was just looking for a place to settle, and when he found this town, it was growing."

Starkweather looked around. "Looks like it might still be growing."

They dismounted in front of one of the town's two hotels, went in, and got two rooms.

"Your friend the sheriff, he going to make a comment about my badge?"

"Probably," Clint said. "Hey, you knew what you were doing when you decided to wear an iron badge. If it bothers you, then start wearing tin."

Starkweather's attitude had softened with each week they rode together. Lately, their relationship had become sort of big brother–little brother.

"I'm not going to wear tin," he muttered.

"Then don't complain when somebody makes a comment," Clint said, flicking the iron badge with a fingernail.

He handed Starkweather his key. "Take the horses over to the livery."

"It's your turn," Starkweather argued.

"No, it's your turn," Clint said. "I did it last time."

"No, I did it last time."

"You sure? Go on," Clint said. "Get going."

"What are you going to do?"

"I'll drop your gear off in your room for you, and then I'll go and see Tom. You meet me at the sheriff's office, and then we'll get something to eat."

"Okay," Starkweather said. "Fine. But if that monster of yours tries to bite me . . ."

Actually, Starkweather and Eclipse had formed a good relationship. The big Darley hadn't tried to bite him in weeks.

Clint walked into the sheriff's office without knocking. Tom Dockery had his back to the door as he pinned some wanted poster to a board on the wall. He was wearing his gun.

"Back to the door, Dock," Clint said. "That's not good."

"What are you talkin' about?" Dockery said. "I knew you were in town before you even got off your horse."

"That a fact?"

Dockery turned around and grinned at Clint. The two men closed on each other and shook hands.

"Been a while," Clint said.

"Yeah, what? Two years? Last time you were here?" Dockery asked.

"Well, since you hardly ever leave this place, it'd have to be here, right?"

"Town looks pretty good, right?" Dockery asked.

"It looks okay. And you look pretty good. Younger than when I last saw you, I think."

"Hey, fifty is young," Dockery said. He backed up a few feet. "You look fit. Still on the trail?"

"Still riding."

"Heard you rode in with somebody."

"Yeah, a kid named Dan Starkweather," Clint said. "Wears a badge out of Kansas."

"Starkweather?" Dockery said. "Not kin to Nate Starkweather, is he?"

"His son."

"And he wears a badge?"

"That's right."

"What are you doing with him?"

"He's trying to find his father."

"What for?"

"To bring him in," Clint said.

Dockery looked surprised. "Why are you helping him?"

"Because he was smart enough to ask for help," Clint said. "And if I don't, he'll end up dead."

"That's just like you, ain't it?" Dockery asked. "Minding everybody else's business."

"Seems like I minded yours once or twice."

"Hey, I'm not complainin'," the lawman said. "You saved my life enough times for me to be grateful you were mindin' my business. So, what can I do for you? Far as I know Starkweather and his gang ain't wanted in Arizona."

"No, they're not," Clint said, "but maybe there's some word about them being seen."

"I haven't heard that from any other law in the state," Dockery said.

"Maybe you could send some telegrams?" Clint said. "Ask around?"

"You gonna be in town long enough to get the answers?" Dockery asked.

"We could use a couple of days on real beds," Clint said.

"I guess I can send a few telegrams, then," Dockery said. "Got time for a steak?"

"As soon as the kid gets here," Clint said. "He's meeting me here."

"Great," Dockery said. "What kind of lawman is he?"

"The kind who's still learning," Clint said. "The kind who wants to learn."

"Well then," Dockery said, "I guess he couldn't be ridin' with a better man, could he?"

"Well," Clint said, "I guess he could do worse."

TWENTY-THREE

"Want some coffee?" Dockery asked.

"You still making it weak?"

"Naw," Dockery said, "I finally learned how to make real coffee."

He went to the stove and came back with two cups and the pot. When he poured it out, it was black as sludge.

"Looks good," Clint said.

Dockery sat behind his desk just as the door opened and Starkweather walked in.

"Sheriff Dan Starkweather," Clint said, "this is Sheriff Tom Dockery."

"Glad to meet you, Sheriff," Starkweather said.

Dockery shook hands with Starkweather, and the badge caught his eye.

"An iron badge," Dockery said. "That sounds like a good idea."

Starkweather looked at Clint.

"I didn't mention it," he said, spreading his hands.

"Does it get heavy?" Dockery asked.

"Sometimes."

"Well," Dockery said, "I guess they all get heavy, sometime. Come on, who wants a steak?"

"I want a thick one," Starkweather said.

"Me, too," Clint said.

"Good," Dockery said, grabbing his hat. "Follow me."

Dockery led them to a nearby restaurant.

"Best place in town to eat," he said. "Only opened a few months ago. I know the owner."

When they walked in, a handsome woman with blond hair came walking over with a smile on her face. The smile transformed her, made her beautiful.

"Thanks for bringing me more customers, Tom," she said.

"Justine Thorn, this is my friend Clint Adams and his friend Dan Starkweather."

"I'm happy to meet you both," Justine said.

"The place looks busy," Dockery said.

"Always a table for the law, Tom," she said. "Come on."

She showed them to a table in the rear.

"Enjoy your dinners. Take my advice and have the steak."

"That's what we're here for, Justine," Dockery said.

"Welcome to town, gents," she said. "Your waiter will be right with you."

"Did Clint tell you who I am?" Starkweather asked.

"Sure," Dockery said. "Who you are and what you're doin'."

"Can you help?"

"Tom's going to send some telegrams to other lawmen in Arizona, to see if anyone has seen Nate and his boys."

"But they're not wanted in Arizona," Starkweather said. "We already know that."

"That doesn't mean they're not known," Dockery said. "Maybe somebody saw them. That would point you in a direction."

The waiter came over and Dockery ordered three steak dinners and three beers. Starkweather remained silent while the two old friends caught up.

When the waiter came with their steaks, they all remained quiet while they attacked their meals. Halfway through, Justine came over to see how they were.

"Sit with us awhile," Dockery said.

"Well," she said, "Just until I'm needed elsewhere."

She sat across from Dockery, between Clint and Starkweather. She looked at Clint.

"You're name is familiar to me," she said. "Have we met?"

"If we had," Clint said, "I'd remember."

"He's Clint Adams, the Gunsmith," Starkweather said. "You must have heard of him."

"The Gunsmith," she repeated. "Well, of course. What brings you to Fenton City, Mr. Adams?"

"Call me Clint, please," Clint said. "I came to see Dock. We've been friends for a while."

"Of course you have," she said. "You must have worked together before."

"That's how it started," Dockery said. "Then we became friends."

"And you?" she asked, looking at Starkweather. "You're a little young to be a lawman, aren't you?"

"Age has nothing to do with it, miss," Starkweather said. "It suits my purpose."

"And you're learning from Clint?"

"We're kind of learning from each other," Clint said.

"Really?" she asked. "Are there still some things the Gunsmith can learn from someone else?"

"We can always learn from someone else, Justine," Clint said.

"I'm impressed," she said.

"Don't let the reputation fool you," Dockery said. "It's never the measure of a man."

"I'll try to remember that," she said. Suddenly, she looked past Clint. "Oh my, looks like an emergency in the kitchen. Excuse me."

She got up and left.

"Quite a woman," Clint said.

"Pretty," Starkweather said. "Kind of old, though. Don't you think?"

"Hey!" Dockery said. "She's younger than me."

"He's twenty," Clint said to Dockery. "I told you that."

Starkweather laughed—probably the first time Clint had heard him do that since they had met.

After supper Dockery told Clint he'd go over to the telegraph office before it closed.

"Meet me in the Cactus Saloon," he said. "It's down the street. Give me about an hour."

"Okay."

"You, too, Dan," Dockery said.

"I think I'm going to go to my room for the night, if you don't mind," Starkweather said.

"You mean these two old-timers are going to last longer than you?"

"I'm afraid so."

"Okay, then we'll see you for breakfast. Your hotel serves a good one."

"Breakfast, then," Starkweather said.

He went back to his hotel. Clint went directly to the Cactus to wait for Dockery.

TWENTY-FOUR

Clint found the Cactus very busy, with gaming tables and a piano player. There were several girls working the floor, serving drinks and sitting on men's laps.

He was able to make a place for himself at the bar, order a beer, and keep a low profile. Nobody paid him any attention—that is, until Dockery appeared and joined him at the bar. Then the curiosity started. Who was the man drinking with the sheriff?

"Sorry," Dockery said. "I seem to have brought you some attention."

"This place still has a shine on it," Clint said.

"Yeah, it's only been open about four months," Dockery said. "It's already put a couple of the smaller saloons out of business."

"This saloon, the hotel, the restaurant . . . the town's really grown."

"It's slowed down now," Dockery said. "People are starting to get used to the new businesses. I think most towns get to a certain point and then really can't support any more growth."

"And you think that's happened here?"

"Well, the mayor and the town council don't think so," Dockery said. "I'm sorta on the fence about it."

"Are you okay with it, either way?"

"Oh, sure," Dockery said. "We get any bigger, I'll just ask for more money in my budget to hire more deputies."

"How many do you have now?"

Dockery grinned and said, "None. Think your kid might want a job farther west than Kansas?"

"I couldn't answer for him, but right now he's concentrating on bringing in Nate Starkweather."

"That's gotta be tough, huntin' down your own pa," Dockery said.

"First, Dan doesn't like referring to Nate as his father," Clint said, "and second, I don't think they've ever really met before."

"Really?" Dockery said. "Well, I guess that would make it easier, but he's still the kid's flesh and blood."

"Guess we'll find out just how much that means when we catch up with him."

"I sent out a half a dozen telegrams, covering a lot of Arizona. If they're in a town somewhere, somebody's gotta notice them."

"Unless they're smart and split up."

"Let's see what kind of responses I get. Another beer?"

"Why not?"

Clint and Dockery remained at the bar long enough for people's curiosity to fade.

"What's going on with you and Justine?"

"Whataya mean?"

"I can see something going on there."

"Well, if anything's going on, it's only on my end," Dockery said. "She's not interested in me. Might be the age thing."

"I thought you said fifty was young?"

"Apparently, not when you're a woman in her thirties," Dockery said. "Why don't you take a run? You're younger than I am, aren't you?"

"I'm not here to discuss my age," Clint said.

"Do you feel like some poker? Faro? Something else?"

Dockery asked.

"No," Clint said, "I think I'm going to take a page out of the kid's book and turn in."

"Hey, the night's young, Clint."

"And as you've been pointing out, you and me are not," Clint said.

"Hey, I never said that!"

Clint slapped his friend on the shoulder and said, "I was reading between the lines."

"Come on, one more beer!"

"Good night, Tom. I'll see you in the morning."

"Early!" Dockery shouted at him.

TWENTY-FIVE

Four men and a guard were on foot, about a mile from Yuma Prison.

"Where are the damn horses?" one of them asked the guard.

"I told you," the guard said. "They're in a clearing over that way. Where's my money?"

"Don't worry," the leader of the four, Herm Jessup, said. "You'll get your money."

He looked over at Willy Castillo, his cell mate for the past six months. They were the ones who had worked out this escape. The other two, Nick Masters and Jerry Foley, were along for the ride. Willy was the only one carrying a gun, which he had taken from the guard. Willy nodded, indicating he knew what to do as soon as they came to the horses.

"You'll get your money," Jessup lied. "Come on, let's go."

Nate Starkweather rolled over in bed and stared bleary-eyed around the room. This was his hotel room. So far, that was okay. Now, where was the hotel? Wait . . . wait . . . Arizona! That was it.

But what town?

He couldn't think of it.

He looked at the woman lying next to him on the bed. She was lying on her stomach, and he could see big breasts flattened out underneath her. She also had a big, fleshy butt, which he liked in a woman. Okay, she'd do, that was fine, but now he couldn't remember if she was a whore he had paid for, or if he'd picked her up somewhere along the way.

Saloon girl? No, she might be built for fucking, but she wasn't built for those dresses the saloon gals wore. She'd always be falling out of the damn thing—which, when he stopped to think of it, wouldn't be so bad.

Well, there was one sure way to find out who she was and where'd he'd gotten her.

He slapped her on her left butt cheek, hard enough to leave a red hand mark. She squealed and rolled over quickly before he could redden the other cheek.

"Hey, that's not the way a girl likes to be woke up!" she complained, rubbing her cheek.

"Are you a whore?" he asked.

"What?"

"I can't remember," he said. "Are you a whore? Did I buy you?"

She got a crafty look on her somewhat fleshy face. She had been pretty once, but now she had a hint of a double chin and her once dewy skin looked more doughy.

"I dunno," she said. "Did we settle on a price?"

"I don't know, either. But I know I don't usually pay a lot."

"Like how much?"

"Five bucks?"

"That sounds good," she said.

"That include a mornin' poke?" he asked.

She spread her legs wide for him, revealing a pink pussy in between heavy thighs.

"Be my guest . . ."

"Nate," he said, sliding his hand down over her belly to her pussy. He touched it with the tip of his middle finger, and she got wet. Apparently, this was a whore who liked her job. "My name's Nate."

She caught her breasts as he slid the entire finger into her.

"I'm Annie," she said.

His dick was hard now, so he got into position between her thighs and shoved it into her. He slid his hands beneath her so he could cup her buttocks—big hands came in handy here—and started fucking her as hard as he could. There was no finesse about the way Nate Starkweather had sex. He did it like he did everything else—as hard as he could, and with no regard for anyone.

Annie didn't care. She wasn't a whore; she was a waitress who had served Starkweather and his boys when they first came to town. When he asked her to come to his room, she figured, why not? Once he mistook her for a whore, she figured it would be some easy money, so she went along with it.

As he pounded into her and she made a point of grunting appreciatively, she wondered what a real whore would charge him for this.

God, she thought, he's like a bull, and is he ever in a hurry.

TWENTY-SIX

Nate Starkweather met Santino at a café down the street from their hotel. Vail had been instructed to keep the other men away from them.

They hadn't pulled a job since the last one, in Lost Mesa. The men were getting antsy, as was Starkweather, but he had something in mind.

The only one who wasn't antsy or nervous was the Mex, Santino.

"How do you stay so calm all the time?" Starkweather demanded.

"I have lots of sex, amigo," Santino said. "It takes care of all my extra energy."

"Did you get a whore, too, last night?"

"A whore?"

"Yeah, you know, like that blonde I had in my room?" Nate asked.

Santino laughed.

"What's so funny?" Nate demanded.

"That woman you took to your room last night was a waitress, not a whore," Santino said. "Did you pay her?"

"Well, yeah, I paid her," Nate said. "I asked her if she was a whore and she said yes. Then we settled on a price. And then we had a helluva mornin' poke."

"Well then," Santino said, "the joke is on her."

"What joke?"

"Since she took your money," Santino said, "that makes her a whore now."

Nate Starkweather thought that over and then smiled and said, "Yeah!"

"I don't get it," Paul Evans said. "Do we smell, or somethin'?"

"Yeah," Walker said. "Nate never wants us near him."

"We always end up havin' to eat with you," Ryan said to Vail.

Vail studied all three men.

"So, what, I smell and you don't wanna eat with me?" he asked.

"No, no, Leo," Walker said, "that ain't what we mean at all."

"What about Santino?" Ryan asked. "I don't want to eat with him."

"Why not? Vail asked.

"He's pretty scary."

"Don't let him hear you say that," Walker said.

"Why not?" Vail asked. "He'd like it."

"Why are we talkin' about eating?" Walker demanded. "When do we pull another job?"

"Don't tell me you went through all the money from the last bank," Vail said.

"It wasn't that much," Walker said, "especially not for us."

"Are you complaining about your split?" Vail asked. "Maybe you should talk directly to Nate about that."

"Oh, no, not me," Walker said. He looked around the café they were sitting in, to see if anyone was listening, then lowered his voice. "I'm not about to give him a reason to kill me."

"Well then, if you're not willing to stand beside what you say, don't say it. Got it?"

"I got it," Walker said.

"You guys?"

"Yeah, we get it," Ryan said, with Evans nodding.

"Then let's have some breakfast and stop talking about it," Vail said.

Leo Vail ate his steak and eggs without looking at the other three, or talking to them. They chattered between themselves, but that was okay. Even though they made him feel like drawing his gun and killing them all.

He knew he was in good with Nate Starkweather and Santino. But these three could not know that. He was Starkweather's eyes and ears, and would keep him informed about his three hired men. Nate liked to know what people were saying behind his back.

Vail thought that he and Santino and Nate could have pulled a lot of the jobs they'd pulled without these three idiots, but Nate seemed to like keeping them around—though not too close. And it was true that their split was hardly enough, but they knew they were making more money with Nate Starkweather than they'd ever make without.

Vail had been putting his own money in the bank, which he knew was kind of ironic. But his split was usually more than the other three put together, and he banked most of it. Once he had enough . . . well, he'd decide what to do when that time came.

"What are you thinkin' about, Leo?" Walker asked.

"Nothin'," he said. "Shut up and eat."

TWENTY-SEVEN

Clint and Starkweather were sitting in the hotel dining room when Sheriff Dockery came rushing in.

"Sorry I'm late," he said, "but I got a telegram you're going to be interested in."

A waiter came rushing over.

"Sheriff?"

"Did you two order?" he asked.

"Steak and eggs," Starkweather said.

"The same," Dockery told the waiter.

"What's in the telegram?" Starkweather asked. "Has someone seen the gang?"

"No," Dockery said, "I got a telegram from Yuma."

"The town, or the prison?" Clint asked.

"The prison," Dockery said. "There's been an escape. Four men."

"And?" Starkweather asked.

"I'm gonna go and help hunt them down," he said. "I want you two to come with me."

"But we're already hunting somebody," Starkweather said. "Nate Starkweather."

"One of the escapees was Herm Jessup."

"Who's he?" Starkweather looked at Clint.

"Jessup's a killer Dock hunted down and put away back when he was a marshal."

"Well, he can get up a posse and do it again," Starkweather said. "We can't—"

"Is that badge just a joke?" Dockery asked Starkweather.

"What?"

"You are a sheriff, right?"

"Of course—"

"Well then, this is your duty, Sheriff," Dockery said. "We've been recruited to help hunt these men down."

"How many?" Clint asked.

"Four men," Dockery said. "They escaped and took a guard with them."

"And what happened to the guard?" Clint asked.

"Nobody knows," Dockery said. "He's still missing." He looked at Starkweather.

"If you refuse," he said, "you'll have to take that badge off."

"No," Starkweather said, "I need to have this badge on when I find my—when I find Nate Starkweather."

"That's fine," Dockery said. "You can continue looking for him after we've put Jessup and his partners back in Yuma Prison."

Clint looked at Starkweather and raised his eyebrows.

"You're either a lawman, or you're not," he said. "Time to decide."

TWENTY-EIGHT

Clint, Starkweather, and Sheriff Dockery rode south of Fenton City, heading for Yuma and Yuma Prison.

"If we're lucky, they headed south," Dockery said.

"Does Jessup know you're the sheriff in Fenton City?" Clint asked.

"I don't know," Dockery said. "He probably does."

"Then he'd probably head this way, just to get his revenge."

"They'd need guns," Starkweather said.

"They have the guard's gun," Clint said.

"Maybe they're not together," Dockery said. "Maybe Jessup will come this way, but the others will go their own ways."

"Not until they have guns and horses," Clint said. "How many ranches and homesteads are between here and Yuma?"

"Quite a few," Dockery said.

"We'll have to warn them along the way," Clint said.

"I agree with Clint," Dockery said. "They'll stay together until they have horses and guns."

"And what about the guard?" Starkweather asked. "Maybe he'll slow them down."

Dockery and Clint exchanged a glance.

"Okay, that was stupid," Starkweather said. "The guard is dead, right?"

"Right," Clint said.

"Okay," Starkweather said.

"We're comin' up on the Simmons ranch," Dockery said. "We better stop and warn them."

"Why did you have to kill the guard?" Nick Masters asked.

"He lied to us about the horses," Jessup said. "And we paid him. I wasn't about to let him get away with that."

Jerry Foley said, "But now they'll be after us forever. We killed a guard."

"He killed the guard," Masters said.

"It don't matter who pulled the trigger," Willy Castillo said. "They will be searching for all of us."

"Damn it!" Foley said. "I knew this was a bad idea."

Jessup turned to face the other three. They were all on foot, and Jessup had the gun.

"All we have to do is come to a ranch and outfit ourselves," Jessup said. "Then, if you want, you can go back to prison."

"Not me," Castillo said. "I will go where you go."

"And where is that, by the way?" Masters asked.

"To a town called Fenton City," Jessup said. "I got an appointment with the sheriff there."

"Why do you have an appointment with a sheriff?" Foley asked.

"Because when he was a marshal he put me in Yuma," Jessup said.

"And you're gonna kill him?" Masters asked.

"Yeah."

"Great," Foley said, "he wants to kill another lawman. They'll never stop looking for us."

"A guard is not a lawman," Jessup said.

"Look," Foley said, "I think I want to go my own way now."

"Me, too," Masters said.

"Well," Jessup said, "I think I'm the one with the gun, and you two are not goin' anywhere until I say so. You wanna argue? Wait until we get some more guns. I don't mind standin' up to both of you."

"Look, Jessup," Masters said, "we're with ya. Don't lose your temper."

Masters and Foley had seen on the inside what Jessup could do when he lost his temper.

"Yeah, Jessup," Foley said. "We're with ya."

Jessup stared at both of them, then looked away. Castillo had walked up ahead a ways and was now coming back.

"Whatawe got?" Jessup asked.

Masters and Foley knew they were going to have to be careful around Castillo and Jessup. Castillo towered over them at six-three, and Jessup was bigger than he was. Either one of them could have torn them to pieces with their bare hands. That Jessup had the guard's gun only meant he might kill them quicker.

"There's a house up ahead," Castillo said. "A corral with some horses. A fallin' down barn. We ain't gonna get much except for maybe a coupla guns and run-down horses."

"And some food," Jessup said. "We don't have a choice. We already passed up the places that had too many hands, too many guns. We're gonna have to hit it."

"There is a family livin' there," Castillo said. "With children."

"Too bad," Jessup said. "Let's go."

He started walking. Castillo went to follow but Masters grabbed his arm.

"We gotta kill kids?" he asked.

Castillo fixed him with a cold stare.

"We have to do whatever Jessup says," the Mexican said.

"Yeah, but killin' kids," Foley said. "Man, I wasn't even inside for murder, just some robberies. I was gonna get out in two years."

Castillo poked him in the chest with a thick forefinger.

"You should have thought of that before you hitched your wagon to Jessup."

"I—I just got excited, ya know?" Foley said. "Caught up in the idea of gettin' out."

Castillo shrugged and started following in Jessup's footsteps.

Foley looked at Masters.

"I know what you mean," Masters said. "I was gonna get out in three."

"What do we do?" Foley asked. "If we kill kids, we'll hang when they catch us."

"I guess we gotta make sure we don't get caught," Masters said.

"We could walk the other way, Masters," Foley said.

"Yeah, then we got the law and Jessup lookin' for us," Masters said. "I'd rather just have the law."

"He might kill us."

"He got us out."

"Yeah, but—"

"Look, Foley," Masters said, "you wanna go, go. I'm stickin' with Jessup."

Masters started walking, and after a few deep breaths, Foley followed.

TWENTY-NINE

"Shit!" Dockery said.

He, Clint, and Starkweather got to the top of a hill and looked down at the Simmons place.

"You said it was a ranch," Clint said.

"It was, once," Dockery said. "I didn't know it got this bad."

"That barn's about to fall down," Starkweather said.

"That might be the least of their problems," Clint said.

"Whataya mean?" Dockery asked.

"Look at the doorway."

Dockery and Starkweather tried to see what Clint was seeing—and then they did. A pair of legs sticking out the open doorway.

"And that corral," Clint said.

"It's empty," Dockery said.

"And the door's wide open," Starkweather said.

"Damn it," Dockery said. "We're too late."

"We better get down there and see the extent of the damage."

They rode down.

* * *

It took five minutes to see that John Simmons was dead, as were his two children, all shot.

"The girl must've been eight," Dockery said. "The boy was a teenager, I think."

"What about a wife?" Starkweather asked. "Was there a wife?"

"There was," Dockery said.

"Jessup and the others must have taken her," Clint said, "and whatever horses were in the corral."

"How close are we to Yuma?" Starkweather asked.

"This is pretty much halfway," Dockery said.

"Why would they pick this place, if there were others between here and Yuma?" Clint asked.

"They probably bypassed the ones that had too many people, too many guns," Dockery said. "This one was ripe for the pickings. They probably got a couple of horses, some food, and some guns."

"And a woman," Starkweather said.

"After being in Yuma," Clint said, "they wouldn't have been able to pass up a woman."

"We have to bury these people," Dockery said. "I'll find a shovel."

"I'm going to take a look at the corral," Clint said. "I might be able to tell how many animals they got."

"Kid, come with me," Dockery said. "Maybe we can find two shovels."

"While we bury them, the escapees are getting further away," Starkweather said.

"First," Dockery said, "these people deserve a burial. Second, I doubt they got prime stock out of that corral. We'll be able to ride them down. And third, your old man's not goin' anywhere. I doubt he's gonna leave the country. You'll catch up to him, eventually."

"You're right," Starkweather said. "I'm sorry."

They went looking for shovels while Clint went to the corral.

As soon as Jessup and the escapees got away from the house, Castillo dismounted and took the woman behind some trees. She'd been riding with him, sitting in front, and all the way she could feel his hardness through his pants. He'd wanted to rape her at the house, but Jessup had stopped him.

"Once we get away from here," he'd said, "she's all yours—and I got seconds."

Castillo pulled the woman down off the horse and carried her into the trees. He found a clearing and put her down. She was wearing a simple, homemade dress that easily came apart in his hands. Her naked flesh excited him even more. He took her all in. She wasn't young, and had a soft belly, but she had full breasts and a bushy patch between her legs. And he hadn't had a woman in five years.

"You want to scream?" he asked.

"I want to die," she said.

"What is your name?"

"Why does it matter?"

"If you do not tell me, I'll hurt you."

"You're going to hurt me, anyway," she said. "You killed my husband, and my children. Do you think I care what you do to me? Come on." She spread her legs for him, so he could see the pink there. "Let's see what a big man you are."

He stared down at her and smiled. He undid his gun belt, dropped it, and his trousers to the ground.

"There," he said, touching himself. "You see how big I am."

She looked at his penis and laughed. "You are not half the man my husband was."

"Your husband?" Castillo asked. "The man who begged for his life?"

"He did not beg for his life," she said. "He begged for mine, and for the lives of my children."

Castillo advanced on her, sat on her legs, and grabbed her breasts. His penis was rigid, and huge. He knew she was trying to insult him so he'd kill her quickly.

"I have been waiting five years for this," he said, "and you will not cheat me out of it."

He got to his knees, spread her legs, and drove himself into her.

Janet Simmons was determined not to scream . . .

Jessup, Foley, and Masters drank some of the water and ate some of the food they'd taken from the house.

"Take it easy," Jessup said. "This food and water has to last."

"Until we come to another house," Foley said.

Jessup looked at the three horses they'd taken from the corral. Only one was a saddle horse, and he'd taken that one for himself. Castillo had taken the best of the other two. That meant Foley and Masters were riding double on the weakest animal.

"These horses ain't gonna last long," Masters said.

"Why did we change direction?" Foley asked. "We shoulda came to another house."

"I didn't want to keep going to Fenton City," Jessup said.

"I thought there was a lawman you had to kill," Masters said.

"And I will," Jessup said, "as soon as I'm properly outfitted."

The only weapon they'd gotten from the house was a Winchester. Jessup was holding on to that and the guard's gun.

"You boys can go your own way now," he said. "You've got a horse, and some food and water."

"This horse? It ain't gonna get us far ridin' double," Masters said.

"If you head for Fenton City, you might find something better."

"What are you sayin'?" Foley asked.

Jessup pointed the rifle at them and said, "I'm tellin' you to go—unless you want a turn at the woman first."

THIRTY

The trail wasn't difficult to follow. Eventually Clint, Dockery, and Starkweather came upon the woman and the two men.

They dismounted, checked the bodies.

"She was raped first," Clint said, looking at the naked woman. "Probably more than once."

"That's Janet Simmons," Dockery said. "So now the whole family is accounted for."

They walked over to the two dead men. Starkweather was standing there, staring down at them.

"Still wearing their prison clothes," he said.

"Jessup killed them, that's for sure," Dockery said. "According to the telegram I got, these would be Masters and Foley."

"And who else?" Clint asked.

"Fella named Castillo."

"You know him?"

Dockery shook his head. "Don't know nothin' about him, except he's probably either friends with Jessup or is of value to him."

"So they killed these two," Starkweather said.

Dockery nodded. "Rather than share the food, horses, clothes—probably the woman—with them."

"If Jessup wants you dead," Starkweather asked, "why did he change direction?"

"He's not ready," Dockery said. "It's that pure and simple. Once he's outfitted, he'll come for me."

"So why don't you just go back home and wait?" Starkweather asked.

Dockery looked at him.

"I'm not trying to be smart," Starkweather said, "I'm just asking."

"Because by the time he got around to me, he might have killed a lot more people—like the Simmons family, and these two."

"That makes sense," Starkweather said.

"We've got to bury these people," Clint said.

"Good thing I brought one of the shovels."

They buried the two men in the same grave, the woman separately.

"If we had the time, I'd take her back and bury her with her family," Dockery said.

"Doesn't much matter," Starkweather said.

"Might matter to her."

"Not anymore." Starkweather turned and walked away.

"That boy got any family other than Nate Starkweather?" Dockery asked.

"Not that I know of."

"That might explain a lot."

They walked away from the graves. This time Dockery left the shovel behind. Clint guessed that if they managed to kill Jessup, Dockery had no intention of burying him.

They mounted their horses.

"If we move fast, we can ride them down," Dockery said. "Even if they have Simmons's saddle horse, they're only gonna be able to move as fast as their slowest animal."

"Clint could probably ride them down faster than we could," Starkweather said.

"That's probably true," Dockery said, "but he'd be outnumbered two-to-one."

"He could take them."

"Jessup's good," Dockery said. "With and without a gun. You're probably right, and I'd probably bet on Clint, but I'd rather we stay together."

"You're the boss," Starkweather said.

"Thanks, kid."

They followed the trail. Clint was not the most accomplished tracker at this point. Dockery was.

"They're ridin' shit horses," he said. "You can see where they've stumbled from time to time."

"You can see that by their tracks?" Starkweather asked.

"You wanna learn something?" Dockery asked.

"Yes, sir."

Clint remained mounted while Starkweather stepped down to take a lesson from Dockery. Clint wasn't looking, but from what he could hear it had to do with the horse stumbling, or leaving scuff marks instead of clear imprints.

Clint kept watch, just in case Jessup and Castillo were lying in wait for them.

"See anything?" Dockery asked Clint.

"Not a thing," Clint said.

"Okay," Dockery said. "Let's get mounted and keep going. We're gettin' closer."

"We are?" Starkweather asked.

Dockery settled into his saddle and said, "We are."

THIRTY-ONE

Jessup and Castillo could not wear the clothes they had found in the Simmons house. The dead man had only been five-foot-ten. None of his clothes, or boots, would fit.

After Jessup had killed Foley and Masters, he had released the third horse. He was riding the rancher's horse, using his saddle. Castillo was on the other horse, riding bareback. His was the animal that was beginning to stumble and would probably soon collapse.

"I'll walk," Castillo told Jessup. "If the horse goes down while I am on it, it might fall on me."

"That's fine," Jessup said. "But that's gonna slow us down."

"I can ride double with you."

"That'll still slow us down."

"Then you go on ahead," Castillo said.

"I think we should stay together, amigo."

Castillo stared up at Jessup. On more than one occasion one had kept the other alive in Yuma Prison. That kind of thing tended to forge a bond between even the most vicious of men.

"Here," Jessup said, handing Castillo the rifle. It was a show of trust that surprised the Mexican. "There must be a posse looking for us by now. We have to find better horses, and more guns. I'll scout on ahead, and when I find something, I'll come back for you."

"Agreed," Castillo said. "I will keep walking."

Jessup nodded, and started his horse forward. Castillo left the other horse where it was—standing, exhausted, with its head down—and started walking. He had taken about three steps when he heard the animal fall.

"We're close," Dockery said.

"How can you tell?" Starkweather asked.

"The tracks are fresher," Dockery said, "and deep, which means the horses are tired . . . and it also helps that I can see one of their horses lying over there."

He pointed. Starkweather saw a barebacked horse lying on the ground, it's sides heaving with its labored breathing.

"Deeper tracks . . . ," he muttered as they rode over to the fallen animal.

Clint dismounted to check the animal.

"He's done in," Clint said. "Won't last much longer."

"If you shoot it, the shot will warn them that we're comin'," Dockery said.

"You don't think they already know that somebody's coming after them?" Clint asked.

"You're right," Dockery said. "Go ahead and do it. It'll give them somethin' to think about."

Clint drew his gun and fired one bullet into the horse's head.

* * *

Just a couple of miles up ahead Castillo heard the shot. He might have been in prison for a long time, but he could still tell where a shot had come from. It was fired from behind him, not ahead, so it hadn't been fired by Jessup.

They had pursuers, and they were getting close. If Jessup did not return with fresh mounts soon . . .

"Did you have to shoot it?" Starkweather asked as Clint remounted. "It didn't have a broken leg or anything."

"That horse had worse than a broken leg," Clint said. "Somebody had just ridden it to death. Once they go down on their side like that, they're done in."

"He's right, Dan," Dockery said. He looked ahead. "Well, now we got two men with one horse. You know what that means."

"They're riding double?" Starkweather asked.

"Not a chance," Dockery said. "First of all, Jessup is about six-four. If Castillo has any size at all, they couldn't ride double. They'd kill the last horse for sure."

"Then what?" Starkweather asked.

"One of them is on foot, probably carrying a rifle they got from the Simmons place," Dockery said.

"The other one has probably ridden ahead, scouting for more food, fresh horses . . ."

"Right," Dockery said. "We might just catch up to one of them alone."

"Yeah," Starkweather asked, "but which one?"

"My money says Jessup kept the horse," Dockery said. "If I know him, he's got no intention of comin' back for the other man."

"Maybe not," Clint said. "I've seen even hard men bond in prison."

"Well," Dockery said, "either way, we'll probably come up on whoever's on foot first."

"After that shot," Clint said, "he'll probably take cover and wait for us."

"Tell you what," Dockery said. "I'll scout up ahead of the path here, and you two just keep going. If he's layin' for us, I'll be able to tell."

"Okay, Dock. Watch your back."

"You, too," Dockery said, "and watch each other's back."

Castillo knew there was somebody hot on their trail. He had two choices, keep walking or stop and wait. If he'd had a better rifle, one he was familiar with, he would have decided to wait. But with this weapon, and with Jessup due anytime with fresh horses, he decided to keep walking, stay on the go, and keep an eye peeled both ahead and behind.

When he'd left, Jessup had every intention of returning to Castillo with fresh horses. He really did. But he'd left the Mexican a rifle, left him able to defend himself. More importantly, Castillo would be able to hold off any pursuers, giving Jessup more time to get farther away.

So yeah, he'd had every intention of finding fresh horses and returning . . . but he wasn't going to.

THIRTY-TWO

"It's too quiet," Starkweather said.

"That's not a bad thing."

"It's been too long," Starkweather complained. "I don't like it."

"Look, Dockery's got to travel quietly. Lawmen have to travel quietly, that's why you see very few wearing spurs, or any kind of baubles or . . . whatever."

"The badge is bauble enough, right?" Starkweather asked.

"Right."

"Right," Starkweather said. "I still don't like the quiet—"

He was interrupted by a shot, then a second.

"Okay," Clint said, urging Eclipse into a run, "how's that?"

Starkweather tried in vain to keep up.

It didn't take long for Castillo to realize what a fool he'd been. Jessup wasn't coming back. He may or may not have intended to, but he wasn't.

The Mexican looked around for cover, spotted a big enough boulder, and made for it. He only hoped that when he fired the rifle, it wouldn't blow up in his hands.

If he managed to get out of this, he'd start hunting Jessup—even though he'd never really expected him to come back.

Because he knew *he* wouldn't have.

Dockery spotted the big man, on foot, carrying a rifle. Had to be Castillo. He dismounted, grounded his horse's reins, and crept forward. He knew the Mexican hadn't spotted him, but he was looking for cover anyway. Maybe it had finally occurred to him that Jessup was not coming back for him.

Dockery had been sitting in an office too long. He knew that because he stepped on a stone, twisted his ankle, and announced his presence to Castillo, who fired—twice.

Damn!

It took Castillo two shots to figure out the rifle was pulling to the left. He saw the glint of sun off the lawman's badge, watched him stagger as he fought to keep his balance. He sighted down the barrel, allowed for the pull, and squeezed the trigger . . .

Everything was laid out in front of Clint as he galloped up. Castillo was pointing his rifle at Dockery, who had apparently injured himself. Dockery was trying to keep his balance and get his gun out at the same time, and the big man with the rifle had a bead on him.

Clint drew and fired in one swift motion.

* * *

When the bullet struck Castillo, he had no idea where it had come from. His finger squeezed the trigger of the rifle he was holding, but the shot went wide.

At that moment Dockery regained his balance and drew his gun, but he had no need to fire. He watched as Castillo spun, dropped his rifle, and fell. Then Dockery turned and saw Clint riding down toward him.

"You okay?" Clint asked.

"I'm clumsy," Dockery said. "Stepped on a stone, twisted my foot."

"Bad?"

Dockery put some weight on the foot. "Not so far."

Starkweather came riding over the hill. "Did I miss everything?"

"Pretty much," Clint said. "Wait here, I'll check and see if he's dead."

Clint dismounted, and handed Eclipse's reins to Starkweather. He walked down and checked on Castillo. Even though he knew his shot had gone straight and true, he turned the body over and checked. Castillo had been a big man, but even a big man will always succumb to a bullet in the heart.

He went back to Dockery and Starkweather.

"He's dead," he said. "I guess Jessup went ahead with the horse, like we figured."

"And he probably never intended to come back," Dockery said.

"So he's still ahead of us," Starkweather said.

"Hopefully," Clint said. "He might have changed direction again."

"Doesn't matter," Dockery said. "I can track him."

He stood up, then almost fell. "Ow! Damn, my ankle."

"If you twisted it," Starkweather said, "it's going to swell up."

"Should we take his boot off?"

"No," Starkweather said, "the boot will hold the swelling down. We might have to cut if off, eventually, but right now we better leave it on."

"I can ride," Dockery said. "That's not a problem."

"Okay," Clint said, "but what do we do with him?" He pointed toward Castillo's body.

"Can't take the time to bury him," Dockery said. "Besides, we left the shovel behind. Cover him with rocks so the animals can't get to him. We'll pick his body up on the way back and take them both back to Yuma."

"You're so sure we're going to catch him?" Starkweather asked.

"Oh yeah," Dockery said. "We're gonna catch him, because we're not gonna stop until we do."

"But your ankle—"

"Like you said, I'll just leave my boot on until we catch him. We better get moving."

He started for his horse, then stopped.

"I'm gonna need help gettin' on my horse."

THIRTY-THREE

Jessup bypassed several homesteads. He was alone, and there were too many people. He needed another place like the Simmons place—down on its luck, just the family. And he needed it fast. He had to have some more food, a better gun, and a better horse.

That was when he saw the lone rider.

They rode hard, but as someone had said earlier, they could only go as fast as their slowest horse.

"Clint," Dockery said, reining his horse in, "you better go on. That horse of yours is beggin' to run."

"Okay," Clint said. "If I catch up to Jessup, I'll take him."

"Dead or alive, I don't care."

"But Clint's the only one without a badge," Starkweather said. "If he kills him—"

"I'll testify that I deputized him—in fact, that I deputized both of you. Your badge is no good here." He looked at Clint. "Go!"

"I'm going."

* * *

As Clint rode off, Starkweather asked Dockery, "How's your ankle?"

"It feels like it's on fire," Dockery said. "I think I'm gonna need a doctor."

"Is there a town we could stop in?" Starkweather asked.

"We could veer off and go to— No," he said, changing his mind. "We've got to keep going."

"Clint and I could keep going, as soon as we take you to a doctor," Starkweather said. "Your ankle might be broken."

"Damn it!" Dockery swore. "It feels like it's filled with broken glass."

"We should have had this talk before Clint took off," Starkweather said. "Look, I'll take you to the nearest town and then I'll try to catch up with him."

"With that horse of his? You'd never catch him. Look, Pixly is just a few miles east of here. It's a stupid name, but they have a doctor. I can get myself there. You go after Clint."

"Are you sure?"

"Yeah," Dockery said. "I'll feel a lot better once I know Jessup's not running free anymore."

Starkweather could see how much Dockery was sweating, and it wasn't from the weather or exertion.

"Okay," he said. "You head over there and see the doctor. When we're done, we'll come there and get you."

"That's good," Dockery said. "Thanks, Dan."

"Sure, Sheriff."

The two men started off in separate directions.

* * *

Clint knew when he saw the house that this would be Jessup's choice. An isolated house with no sign of working hands. He'd already passed up a couple of ranches that were just too busy.

Jessup's tracks led right to it. Clint just hoped he could get down there in time.

THIRTY-FOUR

Jessup only had to knock on the door. When the man answered, Jessup clubbed him with his gun and forced his way in. The man's wife turned from the stove and screamed, putting her hands to her face. She was younger and prettier than the Simmons woman. Castillo would be upset that he'd missed this.

"Shut up!" he told her, stepping over her fallen husband. "Is there anyone else here?"

"N-no," the frightened woman said.

"Don't lie to me. You got any kids?"

"No, no . . . no children. We don't have any."

"That's good. What's that on the stove?"

"Beef stew."

Jessup's eyes lit up. He could kill them later.

"I picked the right place after all," he said. "Dish me up some of that stew right now! You got any bread?"

She nodded. "Fresh baked this morning."

She looked over at her husband. "Don't worry about

him. He'll wake up sooner or later—sooner if he's got a hard head."

Jessup sat down and smiled. "Let's eat."

Having left Eclipse far enough behind that he wouldn't be seen, Clint approached the house carefully. He ducked down and moved up to one of the two windows in front. When he peered in, he could see a man seated at a table with a woman putting a plate of food in front of him. They could have been a husband and wife if it weren't for the prison grays the man was wearing, and the man's body that was on the floor.

He watched long enough—examined as much of the house as he could from his vantage point—to determine that there was nobody else there.

Jessup had made a huge mistake. He was sitting with his back to the door. He had also put the gun down on the table so he could eat. The bad thing was he had made the woman sit across from him. If Clint kicked in the door, there was a good chance he'd get the jump on Jessup, but the escaped prisoner might grab the gun and point it at the woman. Then there would be a standoff.

He decided to keep watching. If the woman got up to go to the stove, he could make his move.

He wondered if the man on the floor was dead.

"Damn," Jessup said, "this is good, woman. I been eating prison gruel for five years."

"Y-you're an escaped prisoner? From Yuma?"

"That's right," Jessup said, "and there's two things I've missed in those five years—good food and the smell of a pretty woman."

"Oh God," she said, closing her eyes.

"Don't worry, honey," he said, "it ain't gonna hurt. I'm sure what you been needin' out here is a real man." He looked over his shoulder at her husband, who had started stirring.

"What is he, about six feet?"

"What? Oh, yes . . ."

"Good," Jessup said, "then I might find some clothes to fit me."

"Please," she said, "we have no money. Take what you need—clothes, gun, a horse—and leave us alone."

"Honey," he said, "the way you cook and the way you smell, I should take you with me. Well, I guess that'll depend on what kind of ride you give me."

"Ride?"

"Yeah," he said, leering at her, "ride. You know . . ."

"Oh God . . ."

"But first," he said, pushing his bowl at her, "get me some more of that beef." He grabbed his gun. "I'll just make sure your hubby don't interrupt us."

When Jessup grabbed his gun, Clint knew he had to move now or the other man was dead. At least the woman was at the stove.

He ran to the door, drew his gun, and kicked it in.

As the door slammed open, the woman screamed. Jessup looked up and saw the man in the doorway. He lifted his gun, but suddenly he felt a pain in his chest, and the man in the doorway lifted his gun . . .

. . . or was that the other way around . . .

* * *

Clint fired one time. The bullet hit Jessup in the chest. The man staggered, frowned at Clint, and then fell over, landing on the other man.

The woman kept screaming.

THIRTY-FIVE

Clint was dragging Jessup's body out of the house when Starkweather rode up.

"I keep missing all the action," he said to Clint.

"You've got to get a better horse."

Starkweather dismounted. "Dead?"

"Yup."

"Inside?"

"Husband and wife," Clint said. "They're okay. Where's Dock?"

"His ankle was pretty bad. I convinced him to go to a doctor."

"Where?"

"A town called Pixly?"

"What a stupid name for a town."

"That's what he said."

"Okay," Clint said, "we might as well take Jessup to Pixly and dump him in Dockery's lap."

"And then what?"

"And then we go back to town and see if any of those telegrams he sent panned out." He put his hand on Starkweather's shoulder. "We go back to looking for your father."

When they got to Pixly, Dockery was hobbling around with a crutch.

"The doctor says it's not broken," he said. "And yeah, he had to cut my boot off."

Pixly was a small town that had come to terms with that fact. They didn't have a lawman. Sheriff Dockery was who they went to for that. But they did have a telegraph key.

"I already sent a telegram back to town," Dockery said. "I heard from a friend of mine, Ray Crocker. He's the law in Chandler."

"Was it about Nate?" Starkweather asked.

"Yeah," Dockery said. "He's sure the gang passed through there."

"Does he have any idea where they were headed?"

"He gave me an educated guess," Dockery said. "He knows of a bank with big deposits. He says any gang worth its salt would want to hit it."

"And where is that?" Clint asked.

"Apache Junction."

"How far is that from here?"

"Chandler's about a hundred miles. Apache Junction's a little further east."

"About a hundred miles," Starkweather said. "That's going to take us three days, even if we push. Can't he hold them there?"

"They're gone already."

Starkweather looked at Clint.

"If they're going to hit a bank in Apache Junction, they're going to have to case it first. That'll take some time," Clint said. He looked at Dockery. "He say when they left?"

"Yeah," Sheriff Dockery said, with a smile. "Yesterday."

"Kid," Clint said to Starkweather, "we're four days behind them."

"We better get mounted, then," Starkweather said. "We have some hard riding to do."

"Oh, no," Clint said. "First, you need a better horse."

THIRTY-SIX

Vail was getting tired of placating Evans, Ryan, and Walker. On the one hand, he blamed Nate Starkweather for taking so long to come up with a plan to hit the Apache Junction bank. On the other, these three should know by now that Starkweather always comes up with a plan.

"What's he waitin' for, Leo?" Walker complained.

"Yeah," Ryan said, "it's just another bank."

"It's just another bank with enough in deposits to keep us all healthy for years," Vail said. "And most of that money comes from three ranches. And those three ranches have each put a man in the bank to guard it."

"So what? They're ranch hands, right?" Evans asked. "Let's just take 'em."

"Plus, there's a sheriff and two deputies," Vail said. "Did any of you geniuses know that?"

"Well . . . sure," Walker said grudgingly.

The four of them were sitting in the Ace High Saloon, where'd they spent most of their time the past two days.

"Nate will let us know when he's ready to go," Vail said. "Just drink your beer."

Nate Starkweather and Santino were sitting in a small café across the street from the bank. They had taken a table by the window and ordered coffee.

"The men are getting restless," Santino said. "According to Vail."

"Leo will keep them in line," Starkweather said. "You notice somethin' about these three men from the ranches?"

"What?"

"There are only ever two inside the bank at a time," Starkweather said. "They got their own little schedule they're keepin' to."

"Where does the third man go?" Santino asked.

"That's what you're gonna find out today," Starkweather said. "And there goes one of 'em."

"You want me to follow each of them when they leave?" Santino asked.

"That's right."

"And you don't think a Mexican followin' three white men is gonna be noticed?"

"Santino," Starkweather said, "anybody ever tell you that you don't look so Mexican?"

"No, amigo, no one has ever told me that."

"Do the best you can."

Santino stood up, started to go, then stopped.

"Wait," he said. "You want them to see me."

"Let's just say I wanna give them somethin' to think about," Starkweather said.

"Amigo," Santino said, "does it not hurt your brain to always be thinkin'?"

"Yeah, amigo," Starkweather said, "but it hurts so good."

In two days Starkweather had figured out the schedules of the three men in the bank, and of the three lawmen. He was pretty sure if his men did what they were told, they'd be able to take this bank. They only had a day left, because he didn't want to be in town for three days. So far no one had seen him and Santino with Leo Vail or any of the others.

Tonight he'd explain the plan.

Tomorrow was the day they'd get rich—only some of them would stay rich longer than others.

Clint and Dan Starkweather camped a day out of Apache Junction.

In Pixly—of all places—they had been able to find Starkweather a little mustang that was managing to keep up with Eclipse, so long as Clint held the big Darley Arabian back some.

"Are you going to figure out a name for that little horse?" Clint asked.

"Why?" Starkweather said. "It's just a horse. I've never understood naming a horse."

"If you don't name him," Clint said, "what will you call him when you're talking to him?"

"I don't talk to my horse, Clint."

Clint shook his head.

"It's a good thing you're not looking for a life on the trail, kid," Clint said. "You can get awful lonely if you don't talk to your horse."

"Why are we talking about this?" Starkweather asked.

"Because you're a little anxious, and I'm trying to keep you occupied."

"Tomorrow could be the day, Clint," Starkweather said. "Tomorrow could be the day I meet my father—and take him in."

"Are you sure you're going to be able to do this, Dan?" Clint asked.

"Oh, I'll do it," Starkweather said. "He's got this coming to him, Clint."

THIRTY-SEVEN

"Everybody know what they got to do?" Nate Starkweather asked.

He looked at each man in turn so that each man had to nod or say yes . . . or no.

"Okay," Starkweather said, "then go."

Ryan, Walker, and Evans left the saloon, while Starkweather, Santino, and Vail stayed.

"What gives, Nate?" Vail asked.

"You, me, and Santino are gonna take the bank," Starkweather said.

"And those three?"

"They're gonna be our distraction."

"So then . . ."

"Only the three of us are going to get away with the money," Santino said.

"Do you have a problem with that, Leo?" Starkweather asked.

"No, Nate," Vail said. "No problem. I was gettin' tired of hangin' around those fellas anyway."

"Good," Starkweather said. "Let's give them some time to get into trouble, and then we move."

Three hours later Clint and Dan Starkweather rode into town and found it in turmoil. People were running in the streets, and there were still bodies.

"We made up a lot of time," Clint said.

"And we still missed them," Starkweather said bitterly.

"But not by much, from the looks of things," Clint said. "We better find a lawman so we can find out what happened."

When they stepped into the sheriff's office, it was crowded with men who were shouting.

"Okay, okay," a man called, waving his arms, "settle down."

Clint and Starkweather took up a position in the back and waited. The man commanding attention was wearing a badge.

"Look, we all know what happened today," the sheriff said. "I lost my two deputies, and three men were killed at the bank."

"And how many of the gang got killed?" someone shouted.

"Three," the sheriff said.

Clint and Starkweather exchanged a glance. Which three? they wondered.

"I need men to volunteer for a posse," the sheriff said.

"Chasing these men down is your job, Sheriff, not ours," someone shouted.

"And you better get to it!" another man yelled.

"Look, we figure three men got away with the money," the sheriff said. "You expect me to track them down alone?"

"Like we said," someone called out, "that's your job."

"Fine," the lawman said. "I better leave right away. If you're not gonna volunteer, then get out."

It didn't take long for all the men to leave the room. The sheriff grabbed a rifle off his gun rack, turned, and saw Clint and Starkweather.

"Who are you?"

"My name's Clint Adams, Sheriff," Clint said, "and this is Sheriff Starkweather, from Kansas."

"What's a sheriff from Kansas doin' here?" the man asked.

They had a clear view of him now, saw that he was in his late forties, with a square jaw and short, gray hair.

"Tracking your bank robbers," Starkweather said. "At least, the gang we think robbed your bank."

"And what gang was that?"

"Nate Starkweather's gang."

The man's eyes narrowed. "You sure?"

"Pretty sure," Clint said. "Can we see the three dead men? Maybe that'll tell us something."

"Be my guest," the sheriff said. "Over at the undertaker's. Come on."

On their way to the undertaker's office, they found out the sheriff's name was Franklin.

"Sheriff," the undertaker said as they walked in.

"Let these two see the dead men."

"Of course. This way."

They followed the diminutive undertaker into a back room, where all three men were laid out on a table—one table. They were almost stacked.

"Know 'em?" Franklin asked.

Clint and Starkweather took a look. It was Starkweather who might have been able to recognize his father, if he'd been there.

"No," Starkweather said, "he's not here."

"Who's not there?" the sheriff asked.

"Nate Starkweather," Clint said. "And none of these men are Mexican, so Santino's not here, either." He looked at Franklin. "How many got away?"

"Three."

"With how much money?"

"A lot," Franklin said. "Three of our biggest ranchers had their payroll in there. They each supplied a man to guard the money."

"What happened to those three men?"

"They're dead."

"How'd you get these three?"

"I believe they were sent as a diversion. They came barging into my office while I was there with my deputies."

"They just happen to break in while you were all there?" Starkweather asked.

"They didn't just happen to," Clint said. "Like the sheriff said, Starkweather sent them in as a diversion, while he, Santino, and his other man hit the bank."

"How is it you know that Starkweather's not here?" the sheriff asked Dan Starkweather.

"That's easy," Starkweather said. "He's my father."

THIRTY-EIGHT

The three men left the undertaker's office and stopped out front.

"You fellas better tell me everything," Franklin said.

"Why don't we do that while we ride, Sheriff?" Clint asked.

"You fellas are gonna ride with me?" the man asked. "Be my posse?"

"The way I see it," Starkweather said, "you're gonna ride with us. We've been looking for him for weeks. This is the closest we've been."

"Three hours," Franklin said. "You missed by three hours."

"If we're that close," Clint said, "we'd better get started."

"Are you with us, Sheriff?" Starkweather asked.

"As long as you tell me everythin' while we're ridin'," Franklin said.

"We'll do that," Clint said.

Franklin pointed and said, "And you can start with that crazy badge."

* * *

By the time they'd ridden two miles, they had filled Sheriff Franklin in. Also in that time Clint had picked up the trail of three horses. And he found the print of the boot with the worn-down heel.

"We're on the right track," he said, mounting up again.

"These men killed both my deputies, and one of the guards in the bank," Franklin said. "When we catch them, they're mine."

"You can have Santino and the other one," Starkweather said. "Nate Starkweather is mine, has been for a long time."

Starkweather gigged his horse and moved ahead of them.

"He's gonna take down his own old man?" Franklin asked Clint.

"He says he is."

"What do you think?"

"I don't know," Clint said. "I don't think we'll know until we catch up to them."

"Is the boy any good?"

Clint nodded, and said, "Good enough."

"Hold up," Nate Starkweather said.

They reined in and looked at him.

"This is where we split up."

"Why?" Vail said.

"They'll have a posse out by now," Starkweather said. "We need to give them three trails to travel."

"Fine," Vail said. "Who carries the money?"

Each man had two money bags across his saddle. They were quite full. It was almost as if they each had two small bodies.

"We take two each," Starkweather said. "We'll meet and make the split."

Vail asked, "Why don't we each go our separate way with two bags?"

Starkweather looked at Vail.

"Because each bag doesn't have an equal amount in it," Starkweather said.

"Gotta be close," Vail said.

"You willin' to take that chance, Leo?" Starkweather asked. "The chance that your bags don't have a lot less in them than our bags do? Remember, we got bills in all sizes. What if your bags are filled with small bills, and mine with bygones?"

"I'd rather take that chance, Nate, than the chance that you'll kill me rather than split."

"Why would I do that?" Nate asked.

"You sacrificed Evans, Ryan, and Walker so we could get away," Vail said. "Why not me?"

Starkweather looked at Santino.

"What about you, Mex?" he asked. "You think I'll kill you rather than split?"

"No."

"Why not?"

"Because this is not all the money in the world," Santino said. "If it was all the money in the world, then yes, I think you would."

Nate Starkweather laughed.

"You're good, Santino." He looked at Vail. "He's good, ain't he?"

"Yeah," Vail said, "he's great. What about it, Starkweather?"

"What? Oh, you mean we each keep our bags? No, I

don't think so, Leo. In fact, I think you better drop yours to the ground . . . now."

"I'm not gonna do that, Nate."

"Then you're forcin' my hand."

Vail laughed.

"Don't kid me, Nate," Vail said. "You were gonna kill me from the start."

"No, I wasn't."

Vail was watching Starkweather, so he never saw Santino draw his gun and point it at him.

"But *he* was," Nate said.

Clint, Starkweather, and Franklin came across the body two hours out of Apache Junction.

Clint dismounted and checked the body. "Shot once, in the back."

"So there's two left." Franklin.

"And they split up," Clint said, pointing to the ground.

"Then we split up," Franklin said.

Clint mounted up. "How many money bags did they get?"

"Six," Franklin said, "packed."

"That explains why one of them took this man's horse. To carry the extra bags."

"That'd be Nate," Starkweather said. "He wouldn't trust anyone else with that money."

"So that trail is Nate Starkweather's," Franklin said, pointing, "and this one is the other man's."

"Santino," Clint said. "The Mexican."

"I'm going this way," Starkweather said, pointing to his father's trail.

"I'll come with you—" Clint started, but Franklin interrupted.

"No, I'll go with the kid," he said. "Nate Starkweather planned this whole thing, and he has most of the money. I want him."

"I've already told you, Sheriff," Starkweather said. "He's mine."

"Okay," Clint said, "I'll track Santino, and you two can fight over Nate Starkweather."

Dan Starkweather looked at Clint.

"Sorry, kid, we can't just sit here and keep arguing. They're getting farther away as we speak."

"You can run the Mexican down with your horse," Starkweather said.

"And you can run down Nate, because he's got an extra horse. When a man's leading another horse, he can't go as fast."

"Are we clear, then?" Franklin said. "Starkweather's mine?"

"You can ride with me," Starkweather said, "but nothing's going to be clear until we find him."

"Kid," Franklin said, "don't get in my way."

Starkweather and Clint looked at each other. They both knew that Franklin was no match for Starkweather—for either Starkweather.

"Good luck, boys," Clint said, and started after Santino.

THIRTY-NINE

Sheriff Franklin and Sheriff Starkweather didn't talk much as they concentrated to follow the trail left by Nate Starkweather.

At one point they had to stop. They were on a road that was much traveled, and Nate's tracks were being swallowed up.

"What do we do now?" Starkweather asked.

Franklin dismounted and started to walk the area, staring down at the ground. When he started to walk, leading his horse with him, Dan Starkweather followed.

Suddenly, Sheriff Franklin turned and looked at Sheriff Starkweather.

"He got off the road here. Guess he don't wanna run into anybody."

He mounted up.

As he followed, Dan Starkweather was thinking of how many lawmen he'd traveled with lately, not to mention Clint, and how he was learning something from each of them.

Picking up tracks on a dirt road was easy. Now he

watched as Franklin picked up the trail on hard dirt, rocks, and grass.

Clint tracked Santino across the same type of terrain. He wondered how the two men intended ever to ride into a town carrying those bank bags. At some point they'd have to transfer the money to some normal-looking saddlebags.

It occurred to Clint that if he just followed Santino, and didn't ride him down, the Mexican would lead him to Nate Starkweather. But if Dan Starkweather and Franklin managed to run down Nate Starkweather, there would be no one for the Mexican to meet.

Well, too many cooks spoil the damn broth. If the decision of which way to go had been left to one man, they all might have followed the trail of one in order to be led to the other.

He'd have to make a final decision when he came within sight of the man—whenever that would be.

The bank bags were unwieldy on Nate Starkweather's horse. Castillo had taken Vail's saddlebags, so the Mexican had about six saddlebags stuffed with the bills that had been in two bags. Vail always carried an extra set of bags. He was a man who was usually prepared for anything—until the end. It was too bad they'd had to kill him, but they really had no choice. There was just too damn much money to split. Starkweather would not have even split with Santino, but to tell himself the truth, he wasn't sure he could take the man. He was sure Santino felt the same way. Neither of them wanted to test it out.

So what Starkweather needed was some more saddlebags, and then he'd be able to make the switch. As if in an answer to a prayer, he heard something up ahead. Whatever it was, it wasn't moving. It was somebody . . . singing.

When Franklin and Starkweather came across the camp and the body, they dismounted. An older man had obviously been there. The fire was still going, and there were some burnt beans in a pan. The dead man was a traveling drummer, and off to one side stood his wagon and his team.

"Why would he kill this man?" Starkweather wondered aloud. "He couldn't have been a threat to him."

Franklin had started to walk the camp, and now he stopped and pointed.

"Saddlebags," he said. "Starkweather stole this man's saddlebags. Look, he emptied out the contents."

Franklin walked to the wagon and looked inside.

"There's a pile of clothes in here," Franklin said. "I bet he got a carpetbag, or a trunk, out of here. He could tie that to the second horse."

"If he's got the money in saddlebags, and some other kind of bag, he'll be able to ride into another town," Starkweather said.

"Not close to here," Franklin said. "Not when the word gets out about the bank, and the killings."

"Then he'll keep going and he won't stop until he's crossed the border into . . . somewhere."

"He can go to Utah, Nevada, or California."

"And I'll go right after him."

Franklin frowned. "I can't. At some point, I'll have to turn back. I don't have an iron badge, just this tin one that the people in town gave me. I can't leave them."

"This badge is no different than that one, but when I accepted it they understood what I was going to do. I'm going to track him until I find him."

"Well," Franklin said, "some other lawman won't accept your badge as official, not as long as you're outside of Kansas."

"That's okay," Starkweather said. "This is a symbol that I'm nothing like my father."

"Well," Franklin said, "I'll go with you as far as I can."

"Then let's ride. Maybe we can catch up to him before he crosses one of those borders."

FORTY

When Santino's horse went lame, he cursed everyone he could think of. He had four saddlebags full of money, which were too heavy for him to carry for any distance. He dismounted and checked the horse's left foreleg. It wasn't broken, but the animal was favoring it. Santino figured he could walk, and leave the saddlebags on the horse. First ranch or homestead he came to, he could pick up another horse. Since he had money, he could buy a horse rather than steal one. That would leave no trail.

He grabbed his horse's reins and started walking.

Clint rode Eclipse hard. Every so often he stopped to check the tracks, and knew he was getting closer. When the tracks showed that the horse had gone lame, and the man was now walking, he knew he'd catch up. Finally as the day neared dusk, he saw a man leading a horse up ahead of him. He urged Eclipse on even faster.

Santino heard the horse and turned. He saw the man on the big black coming at him at breakneck speed. He went for his gun, but he could see that he was too late. The man on the horse was fast . . . so fast . . .

Clint gunned Santino down with one shot. Clint leaped to the ground, kicked the man's gun away, and then checked the body. He wasn't dead. He went to the horse and looked in the saddlebags. They were packed with money.

He went back to Santino. He was bleeding and would be dead soon. Clint slapped the man's face to bring him around.

"*Madre de Dios* . . ."

"You're going to be dead in minutes, Santino," Clint said. "Where were you supposed to meet Starkweather?"

"Doctor," Santino gasped, "I need a doctor . . ."

"A doctor can't help you, my friend," Clint said. "You're going straight to hell unless you come clean and help me."

"I—I must pray—"

"No, no," Clint said, "no praying. I'm not going to let you pray until you tell me. I won't leave you alone until you die, and if you die without making your peace with God, you're going to hell."

"God—"

Clint smacked Santino to stop him. "No prayers!"

"M-Mesquite."

"What?"

"Mesquite, Nevada."

Right on the border.

"You better be telling the truth, Santino."

"I—I will pray now . . ."

Clint looked at the wound. The deep color of the blood told him all he needed to know.

"You can start," he said, "but I don't think you have much time left."

"Damn it!" Franklin said.

"What is it?"

"He's doubled back on us," Franklin said. "It looks like he's gonna go west."

"Into Nevada?"

"That's my guess. It'll take him a couple of days or so to get to the border. You'll probably have to cross the border before you catch him."

"Before I catch him?"

"I have to go back, Starkweather," Franklin said. "I wish you luck. Don't try to ride at night. Your horse will step in a chuckhole."

"If Clint and I recover the money, we'll bring it back."

Franklin put out his hand. "I know you will."

The two men shook hands, and went their separate ways.

Starkweather was angry. His father had a three-hour head start, and while there was every indication that they'd catch up to him, he seemed to have widened that gap. Starkweather knew he'd have to camp tonight and start again in the morning. He didn't know the terrain, so he wouldn't go against Franklin's advice and travel at night. He was willing to bet that wouldn't stop Nate Starkweather. He'd travel at night, putting a few more hours between them.

But that didn't matter. Dan Starkweather would continue to follow, and wouldn't stop until he caught up. He figured he was on his own now. Clint was still after Santino. And there was no way Clint could know that Nate was heading for Nevada.

No way at all.

FORTY-ONE

Nate Starkweather poured himself another drink from the bottle he'd bought about half an hour ago. He was drinking it slow while he tried to work on his problem. When he reached the outskirts of Mesquite, he'd realized he couldn't ride into town with all that money—even if it was now in saddlebags and a canvas bag he'd taken from the drummer. The bag was bursting, and the saddlebags wouldn't close all the way. That would arouse too much curiosity. So he'd had to find a place to hide the money, so he could ride into Mesquite, meet up with Santino, and get outfitted. He'd taken a couple of bundles of bills from one saddlebag and put them inside his shirt.

Just why he had decided to keep the meeting with Santino he didn't know. Maybe he was going soft, but he figured he needed somebody to watch his back. Of course, the Mexican might have been happy with the money he had and just kept going. Nate figured to give him a day or two and then be on his way.

But he was nervous about the money. He'd hid it well, but that didn't mean somebody wouldn't stupidly stumble upon it.

So he figured he'd finish this bottle of whiskey, get outfitted, and ride back out to pick the money up, and then head for California.

Just a couple more drinks.

Dan Starkweather had had to weather a few hardships on his way to Mesquite. The fine mustang he'd bought in Pixly stepped in a chuckhole after all, and it wasn't even dark. Just a stupid, unavoidable accident. So he'd had to walk awhile before he came upon a ranch where he was able to buy another horse. That had put him even farther behind Nate Starkweather. But he kept going, using everything he'd learned from Clint and Dockery and Franklin to stay on Nate's trail.

He'd lost the trail just outside of Mesquite, so he was riding into town for two reasons. One, he was thirsty and starving, as he'd run out of water and beef jerky, which Clint had told him to always carry. And two, it was the town closest to where he'd lost the trail, so he had to check to see if Nate was there.

As he rode down the main street of Mesquite, Dan Starkweather had a feeling his search was going to end here. Clint had preached following your instincts for weeks. Well, here it was. His instinct told him this was it. Get off your damn horse and start looking.

He rode past the local sheriff's office and didn't stop. It would take too long to explain what he was doing there, and what the hell kind of badge he was wearing.

Mesquite was not a large town, but there were two hotels and three saloons. He could ask at the hotels, see if Nate had checked in, but what was the use? He would have used a phony name. It was more likely the man was in one of the saloons.

As for how he'd recognize the father he'd never met, his mother had once showed him a tintype of his father as a younger man. From that—and from the instinct Clint had preached to him about—he would recognize Nate Starkweather right away.

He reined in in front of a hardware store, dismounted, and tied the horse off to a post. Then he started walking.

Nate Starkweather was down to the bottom of the bottle. One more drink, and Santino had not yet arrived. So, he had either ridden off satisfied with the money he had in his bags, or he'd been caught.

He poured the last of whiskey into his glass. Oddly, he wasn't feeling the effects of an entire bottle of whiskey. He looked around. Everything was still in sharp focus. He'd deliberately chosen the smallest saloon in town. He and the bartender were the only ones there. Normally, he'd take over the largest saloon in town and dare anybody to do something about it. But in this town he'd wanted to be alone, just him and a celebratory bottle. He was rich, whether Santino showed up with the rest of the money or not.

He was sitting at a back table with his back to the wall, and was about to down the last of his whiskey, when the batwings opened and a young man walked in.

* * *

Dan Starkweather went through the first and second saloons without finding his father. That left the last one, and the smallest, which he was now standing in front of. He thought he'd find a man like Nate Starkweather in the biggest saloon, flashing his newfound wealth, but that wasn't the case.

If Nate was in town, he was in here.

He pushed through the batwings and entered.

Nate Starkweather looked at the man who'd entered the saloon, saw the iron star on his chest, then looked at his face.

The young man approached his table.

"Damn," Nate said. "You look just like your mother."

"You know me?" Dan asked.

"A man knows his own flesh and blood, boy," Nate told him. "How's your mom?"

"She's dead," Dan said. "Died of a broken heart, thanks to you."

"Not my doin'," Nate said. "She knew we was never gonna be together."

"She died because of the legacy you were intent on leaving me."

"I ain't leavin' you nothin', kid. What'd you come here for, to take me in?"

"I've been doggin' your trail for months," Dan said, "and I finally have you."

"That badge for real?"

"It is."

"Then you're just a man with a badge to me," Nate said. "Nothin' more."

"That suits me."

Nate laughed and sat back. "You're gonna shoot your old man?"

"You're just a man with a price on his head to me," Dan said.

Nate and Dan Starkweather stared at each other. Neither had any remorse over what was about to happen. They may have been related, but they felt nothing for each other. For that, Dan could thank his father, Nate. If he'd inherited his mother's gentle heart, this would have been hard.

"You gonna let me stand up?" Nate asked.

"First tell me where the money is."

"Ah," Nate said, "you want the money."

"I want to take it back to the people you stole it from."

"Well, good luck with that," Nate said. "Gonna be hard for a dead man to do that. So, like I said," Nate spread his arms. "Gonna let me stand up?"

"Go ahead," Dan said. "Stand up."

Nate smiled, pushed his chair back, and when he got to a half crouch, went for his gun . . .

Clint was riding into Mesquite when he heard the two shots. He wasn't sure where they had come from, and neither were the other people in town. Some of them came out onto the street to see what they had missed.

When Clint saw Starkweather stagger out of a small saloon, he rode over and dismounted quickly. He caught the boy as he fell off the boardwalk.

"Dan?"

"My chest . . . ," Starkweather said.

Clint looked at his chest, didn't see any blood. But he did see a dent in the iron badge the boy was wearing.

"Clint, h-he beat me."

"He may have beaten you to the draw, kid, but where is he?"

"Inside," Starkweather said. "He's dead."

"Then it doesn't matter if he beat you or not," Clint said. "He's dead. How do you feel?"

"Like a mule kicked me in the chest." Starkweather looked up at him. "How did you get here?"

"I caught up to Santino and killed him. I was taking the money he had back to town when I ran into Sheriff Franklin. He told me that you had continued on, so I gave him the money and let him return it. And I started after you."

"That damn horse of yours," Starkweather said. "You must've flown."

"Just about. Come on, let's get you to your feet. Should be some law along by now."

Clint helped Starkweather to his feet. "Can you stand?"

"Yeah," Starkweather said, rubbing his chest. "Stupid badge saved me."

"Well, now we know why you wore it."

They both saw a man with a badge—a silver badge, reflecting the sun as he ran—coming toward them.

"The money," Starkweather said. "I don't know what he did with the money, Clint."

"I do," Clint said. "I found it outside of town. He stashed it in a dry creek bed."

"I passed that creek bed," Starkweather said. "How'd I miss it?"

"I think you had other things on your mind," Clint said. "Here comes the law."

"I killed him, I guess I'll do the talking," Starkweather said.

"Fine with me," Clint said. "At least when he asks you about your badge, you'll have something new to say."

Watch for

THE TOWN COUNCIL MEETING

332nd novel in the exciting GUNSMITH series
from Jove

Coming in August!

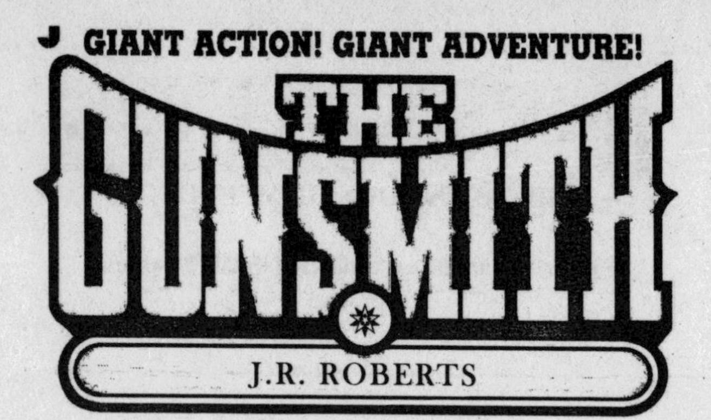

Little Sureshot And
The Wild West Show
(Gunsmith Giant #9)

Dead Weight
(Gunsmith Giant #10)

Red Mountain
(Gunsmith Giant #11)

The Knights of Misery
(Gunsmith Giant #12)

The Marshal from Paris
(Gunsmith Giant #13)

penguin.com/actionwesterns

M228AS0808

LONGARM